Buried Treasures of the Atlantic Coast

Other *Buried Treasures* books by W. C. Jameson

BURIED TREASURES OF THE ATLANTIC COAST

Legends of Sunken Pirate Treasures,
Mysterious Caches, and Jinxed Ships
—From Maine to Florida

W.C. Jameson

August House Publishers, Inc.
LITTLE ROCK

Published 1998 by August House, Inc.,
P.O. Box 3223, Little Rock, Arkansas, 72203,
501-372-5450.

Printed in the United States of America

10 9 8 7 6 5 4 3 2 1

LIBRARY OF CONGRESS CATALOGING-IN-PUBLICATION DATA
Buried Treasures of the Atlantic Coast/ W. C. Jameson
p. cm.
Includes bibliographic references
ISBN 0-87483-484-8
1. Atlantic Coast (U.S.)—History, Local—Anecdotes
2. Treasure-trove—United States—Atlantic Coast—Anecdotes
I. Title
F106.J28   1997
974—dc20   96-38773

President and publisher: Ted Parkhurst
Executive editor: Liz Parkhurst
Project editor: Suzi Parker
Cover design and maps: Wendell E. Hall

AUGUST HOUSE, INC.   PUBLISHERS   LITTLE ROCK

Contents

Introduction

Not too many years ago, I was walking along the shore of an Atlantic Coast beach when I made an important discovery.

At my feet in the bright sands, an even brighter gleam caught my attention. On examination, I discovered an eight-*reale* Spanish coin, an irregular silver circle hundreds of years old that probably washed up from some long-forgotten shipwreck. Carefully brushing the sand away from the slightly corroded surface, I gazed upon not just a piece of eight, but a piece of history with which I had long been trying to make a connection.

Several weeks before my shoreline visit, I invested hundreds of hours of time visiting libraries and researching tales and legends of pirates, buccaneers, and marauders, who sailed up and down this same coast, attacking merchant vessels and pillaging small communities. I sought information on the hundreds of shipwrecks that once carried great treasures and now laid tantalizingly close to the coast. I interviewed dozens of people, many who claimed to know the truth behind the pirate and shipwreck legends and the facts connected to the many lost and buried treasures associated with them.

Fascinated, I've sat for hours listening to Atlantic Coast residents recall the tales they heard so often as youngsters growing up in the area. I spoke with so many historians and members of historical societies that I lost count. I visited at least twenty museums and viewed numerous private collections, all containing artifacts of that long ago time. For instance, at the

Ocean City Lifesaving Station Museum, a variety of treasures—
two, four, and eight Spanish *reale* pieces, so-called pillar dollars
mined in Mexico and minted in Potosi and Bolivia bearing the
image of Charles III—are on display in glass cases. Many of these
finds were discovered on Coin Beach in Maryland, one of the
most treasure-laden beaches on the Atlantic Coast.

I learned much during my interviews and visits, but most of
it remained somewhat intangible until I picked up the coin.
Here in my hand, I had established the link between today and
the yesteryear of pirates, sunken ships, and lost treasures.

Pirates have existed since the time the first civilizations took
to the seas. Just as outlaws and bandits held up stagecoaches
and ore wagons on land, the pirates of the high seas preyed upon
merchant vessels and passenger ships. Victims were sometimes
killed, but the pirates always took the wealth carried in the
passengers' pockets or stored in the safes and holds of the ships.
For thousands of years, this kind of predation took place in the
five oceans of the world, and untold treasure worth millions of
dollars was stolen. Much of that incredible wealth was buried
along the Atlantic Coast of the United States. The coast's
continental shelf is so littered with shipwrecks that they are
often noted on maps of the region.

Treasure along the Atlantic Coast ended up lost or buried
because of factors other than pirates seizing and burying booty.
Some ships, manned by pirates, were attacked and sunk by
American or British warships. Other ships were lured by false
lights, which lookouts believed glowed from other ships. Actually, the lights came from bandits on shore, and the ships,
believing the twinkling lights were out in the ocean, ended up
running aground. Once a vessel was lodged on the rocky shoals,
a short distance from the coastline, the robbers rowed out to the

8

ship and stole its cargo. Often, the bandits buried the treasure and never returned to retrieve it.

Other treasure-laden ships plying coastal waters from Mexico and South America, where they were loaded with riches from those countries' mines, to Europe occasionally sailed fatally into hurricanes and other violent ocean storms. More often than not, it was these violent storms, and not piracy, that plagued the wind-powered galleons as they attempted the ocean crossing.

A large number of sunken ships belonged to Spain during this time and often made the trip across the ocean to that country. During the six decades when the Spanish were heavily mining and shipping gold and silver, hundreds of ships safely made the crossing. Others, however, never finished the course. The weather turned dangerous, and these vessels carrying coins, ingots, precious stone, finely crafted jewelry, and valuable church relics sank to the ocean bottoms, coming to rest on the continental shelf, sometimes only a few hundred yards from the shores.

Since the times when pirates' only banks were remote caches on uninhabited barrier islands and unpopulated shores, thousands of storms have battered the coast. In some cases, these storms have washed away several feet of beach sand, exposing treasure chests loaded with coins or kegs packed with gems. In other cases, the storms have scattered treasures across the beach for hundreds of feet. The powerful, swirling currents of the sea, often driven by frequent storms that blow across the coastal region, have carried coins and other artifacts from the rotted remains of sunken shipwrecks to the coastal beaches where they were deposited beside shellfish and ocean debris.

However, the waters of the Atlantic Ocean are believed by many to protect the treasures that dot the continental shelf. Most of the lost shipwreck treasures have never been found, and many that have been located have been impossible to examine because of the strong tides. Some of these caches and deposits have been discovered through the years. Indeed, thousands of gold and silver coins with centuries-old mintage have been discovered on Atlantic Coast beaches. Occasionally, huge treasures, long trapped in the sunken hulks of these sailing ships, are recovered.

With the discovery and retrieval of these riches, we are also recovering crucial artifacts, reminders of a life and time long vanished, from important historical eras. The value, both monetarily and historically, is inestimable.

Throughout the past hundred years or so, a few men and women have become wealthy discovering and recovering lost, sunken, and buried pirate treasure. Scholars, however, agree that only a small percentage of the total amount of loot buried or sunk with the ships has yet to be recovered.

Because many documented and undocumented sinking and caches have never even been found, the potential of great treasure lying just below the sand's surface or in several feet of water a short distance offshore lures many hunters.

The draw to lost treasure can be irresistible, and many people easily succumb to it. Some men devote their entire lives to the search for it, but only a few are truly successful. Despite the relatively small numbers who actually find a grand treasure, thousands continue to comb the beaches almost daily for coins and caches or search the continental shelves for the remains of long-sunken treasure-bearing ships.

At some point in their lives, these searchers have heard the stories—sunken treasure tales, pirate booty legends, and the mysteries behind long-lost maps, with an "X" pointing to a secret spot, found in musty attics— that lead to a buried chest brimming with coins. Entering the realm of folklore and legend, these tales fascinate and often provide unending inspiration for in-tense searches and dreamy hopes of discovery. The tales also bubble with intrigue. Many people can simply find adventure between the pages of a book; others thrive on the actual search—the quest—for lost riches.

Swept up in high seas drama and the longing for riches, it is easy to imagine the ocean wind in one's face during deck watch and hear the flap of the canvas sails as they fill with wind. Time and again as I researched these tales from the days of yore, I could almost hear the crunch of beach sand beneath the feet of pirates carrying a loot-filled chest to some hiding place near the shoreline. In my nightly dreams, I held gold and silver coins, counting each glistening piece, and gazed upon jewelry and precious stones seized by the brigades.

And now, the beginning of your own adventure starts in these pages.

MAINE

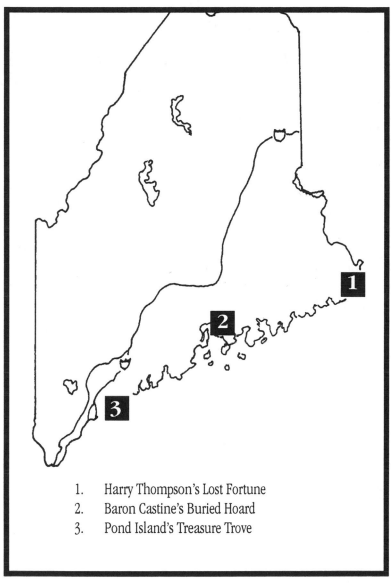

Harry Thompson's Lost Fortune

Pirate Harry Thompson was considerably lesser known than Black Bellamy, but like his counterpart he has long been associated with a huge buried treasure in the Machias Bay area.

Thompson, along with an accomplice known only as Starbird, crossed the Atlantic Ocean from America to Europe and Africa several times, preying on defenseless merchant vessels. It is estimated that the two brigands plundered at least twenty-four ships over a span of eleven years. Several times a year, the two returned to Machias where they buried the loot on a patch of land located on the east side of the bay.

Thompson, unlike other pirates of his day, was not given to braggadocio and maintained a very low profile. For the most part, the commanders of ships sent out by the British and French governments to end pirate activity in the Atlantic never heard of Thompson, and it is believed that many of his piracy acts were often blamed on other and better-known brigands.

Along with a secretive nature, Thompson was rather frugal and spent very little of his fortune on anything except refurbishing and maintaining his ships. Most of what he possessed he buried, and in time the pirate accumulated a sizeable hoard.

As Thompson grew older, he gradually lost his passion for piracy and began spending more time in the home he built near Machias Bay. As his days of sailing the high seas and plundering other ships drew to a close, Thompson's long-time friend and partner, Starbird, loaded a fortune in booty onto a sailing vessel and departed, as he told his companion, for the safety of South America. Thompson never saw him again. In time, Thompson sent for his young wife, son, and two daughters who were living in England, and when they arrived he moved them into his quarters.

With the help of servants, Thompson and his family farmed a sizeable piece of land and sold their harvest to area merchants and residents. No one was aware that this always-smiling and kind family man was once a notorious and feared pirate.

On occasion, Thompson vanished for one or two hours at a time and went to his secret cache, eventually returning to the house with a pouch of gold coins. All he ever explained to his wife and children was that his fortune was buried somewhere on the farm, but he steadfastly refused to reveal the location.

As Thompson's children grew up, the old pirate knew that someday they would inherit his fortune. Wary of revealing the location outright, he began to scratch crude directional markings, cryptic signs indicating the location of his valuable horde, on stones and trees on and around his property.

One evening when he was a very old man, Thompson sat down at a table to sketch a map on a piece of parchment that showed the location of his great treasure. With a feeble hand shaking with age, he dipped the pen into the ink well and undertook a sketch of his farm. After outlining the boundaries of his property and drawing vague representations of the house and barn, Thompson's heart suddenly gave out and he collapsed to the floor, dead.

A few years later, Thompson's widow died and the children were sent to live with neighbors. Thompson's son, Willis, did not take to his foster parents and at the first opportunity ran away and took a job on a merchant ship.

For nearly twenty-five years, Willis earned his living working on ships carrying cargo between the United States and England, and by the time he was forty, he was piloting his own vessel and signing documents "Captain Willis Thompson."

Willis eventually tired of the sea and, after some consideration, decided to retire to the family farm near Machias Bay. After obtaining legal title to the land, Willis moved into the farm's original dwelling.

Among the family belongings stored in the old house, Willis discovered a small chest containing papers and various documents. Examining the contents long into the evening, Willis chanced upon a note written by his father that alluded to the buried pirate trove somewhere on the family property. On the yellowed page, Henry Thompson indicated that he had marked stones and trees with clues to help locate the treasure. Fascinated, Willis Thompson decided to search for his late father's buried cache.

The first obstacles encountered by Willis were the clues themselves—his father's carvings and directions were all but undecipherable! No matter how many different ways Willis interpreted the line drawings and cryptic notations, he could make no sense of them whatsoever.

After several weeks of failing to interpret his father's markings, Willis knew there was only one thing to do. Convinced of the great treasure's existence somewhere on the farm, he decided to deep-plow the soil in the hope of locating it. Fashioning a custom-made plow that would penetrate about two feet below the surface, Willis hitched the contraption to two stout oxen and undertook the tilling of the large field.

Working as long as twelve hours a day for weeks at a time, Willis plowed the field with a fierce determination, believing all the while he was only inches away from striking the treasure.

During the years Willis was away at sea, numerous settlers moved into the Machias Bay region and tiny communities had developed. Once remote and somewhat isolated, the old Thompson farm was now almost ringed by neighbors, and, on a daily basis, throngs of onlookers gathered at the edge of the field to watch Willis negotiate the odd-looking plow back and forth. Now and then, the former sea captain paused and eagerly examined the soil around the plow, and when he did, the watchers waited silently and breathless, hoping to witness the discovery of the treasure. More often than not, however, Willis only turned up an old iron kettle or rusted tool.

For nearly six years, Willis Thompson plowed the old field but never found his father's vast fortune. Eventually, the residents in the nearby communities began to think Willis was daft, obsessed, and really unable to relinquish pursuit of what they came to believe was only a dream.

But Harry Thompson's buried treasure was no dream. Most who have studied the Thompson story firmly believe the old pirate cached millions in gold, silver, and jewels—a fortune that to this day still lies buried somewhere on the old Thompson homestead somewhere above Machias Bay's eastern shore.

Baron Castine's Buried Hoard

The community of Castine, Maine, located on a spit of land projecting out into a northerly portion of Penobscot Bay, was first settled in 1629 by British immigrants. Since then, its history has often been clouded with violence and bloodshed, but Castine's past also beams with a tale of a lost, but not forgotten, buried treasure that once belonged to a French nobleman.

Jean Vincent de l'Abadie grew up a boisterous and uncontrollable youth in France. By the time Jean Vincent was twenty years old, his parents tired of enduring the continued embarrassment brought upon them by their rebellious son. Their response was to provide him with a stipend and ship him off to Canada. Just before placing the young Jean Vincent on a vessel bound for the New World, his father, a powerful and influential baron, secured a lieutenant's commission for him in the Canadian militia.

On arriving in Canada, young Jean Vincent immediately took to military life, actually enjoyed it, and was placed in charge of a frontier battalion assigned to protect a portion of Quebec from marauding Indians.

Jean Vincent was aware that his family owned a large parcel of land near the mouth of the Penobscot River, where the stream empties into the Atlantic Ocean. After acquiring an extended leave of absence from the army, he decided to travel to the location and examine it. After making most of the journey by canoe down the Penobscot River, Castine finally arrived at the tiny village of Pentagoet. Originally an important center of trade between the British and area Indians, the French, who coveted what they believed to be a strategic location, attacked the village and held it for several years. In 1688, British forces regained it after a brief skirmish, only to lose it once again to the French about a year later. It was shortly after the second possession by the French that Jean Vincent arrived at Pentagoet. He immediately fell in love with the location and decided to return and settle once he had fulfilled his military obligation.

A few years later, Jean Vincent mustered out of the Canadian militia, moved to Pentagoet, and promptly renamed it after his family. The Frenchman, more sympathetic toward the Indians than antagonistic, established friendly relationships with the neighboring tribes and conducted a brisk trade business. The Indians thought so highly of Jean Vincent that they made him an honorary chief.

Around this time, young Jean Vincent learned of his father's death and of his inheritance—the title of baron. To celebrate, he married the daughter of one of the most powerful chiefs of the Penobscot tribe, further cementing his alliance with the natives.

As a highly successful trader and businessman, Baron de St. Castine amassed a small fortune in gold coins that he kept buried in a secret location known only to himself and his young daughter.

One day, Castine returned from an extended trapping expedition only to learn that his settlement had been overtaken by Flemish pirates who had killed and imprisoned most of the Indians. Leading a strong resistance force, Castine, with help from his Indian friends, quickly and effectively expelled the invaders.

On other occasions, British militia attacked the settlement, and, occasionally, nearby New Englanders raided it. One of the most vicious assaults on the community came from an army of Massachusetts and Maine volunteers under orders from then Governor Sir Edmund Andros. The attack was so ferocious that the inhabitants of Castine were forced to flee into the woods. When they returned several days later, they discovered that Andros's troops had plundered much of the community's wealth. Baron Castine's personal fortune, however, was still intact in his secret hiding place.

In retaliation, Baron Castine organized an army of Abanaki Indians and attacked, looted, and burned several hostile villages along the coast, even as far away as New Hampshire.

Relationships between Castine and British settlers eventually grew so intense and hostile that the Baron decided to construct a log and rock palisade around a portion of the settlement that included his trading post and dwelling. Several large cannons were mounted in strategic positions with anticipation of future raids.

Baron Castine's precaution proved ineffective when a strong British force led by Major Church stormed and captured the village in 1704. One reason given for the swift defeat was that Castine, a skilled fighter and strategist, was not even present. He was, at the time of the raid, in France conducting family business.

Several Indians were killed during the attack, and Castine's daughter, fearing the British would discover her father's large cache of gold coins, decided to remove the treasure to a safer location. After digging up the coins, she placed them in stout leather pouches, secured them to two horses, and led the animals away from the fighting under the cover of darkness.

For most of the night, the daughter trekked through the dense woods along a winding route that took her in a generally north-eastern direction. As the rising sun began to brighten the forest landscape, Castine's daughter realized she was very close to the shore of The Narrows, a portion of the Bagaduce River just northeast of Grindles Eddy. She spied a large boulder nearby, and next to it she scooped out several holes where she buried the gold coins.

Within an hour, British soldiers, who had followed Castine's daughter, captured her and placed her in confinement at Portsmouth. She never returned to the region to retrieve the money. Nor did Baron Castine, who died in France only a few days later.

Many who knew about the existence of Baron Castine's treasure wondered what happened to it, but with time the subject faded from the memories of area residents. Then, in 1849, a farmer named Stephen Grindle along with his son, Sam, were dragging logs along the banks of the Bagaduce River to a spot where they were building a cabin. Needing to rest the mules, which were pulling the heavy logs, Grindle ordered a halt near a large rock located about ten yards from The Narrows. As Grindle and his son rested against the boulder, the farmer noticed several gold coins in one of the ruts cut by a dragged log. For the rest of the day, father and son searched the area for more coins, eventually finding twenty.

Excited by their discovery, the Grindles rode to their nearby farm and returned with picks and shovels. During the next several weeks, the two men dug up a total of two thousand gold coins.

Did the Grindles retrieve all of Baron Castine's treasure? Experts who have studied this tale believe that the two men actually only uncovered a small portion of the cache. Unfortunately, no one can remember the exact location where the Grindles found the money, and though treasure hunters have combed this shore of The Narrows for more than one hundred years, the rest of Baron Castine's treasure remains lost.

Pond Island Treasure Trove

An unspectacular rocky isle, less than one-half mile long by a quarter of a mile wide, sits in Portland's Casco Bay, just east of Bailey Island. A pond, which is located in the middle of the island, bestowed the body of land with its simple name—Pond Island. But little did anyone know that one day, one of the largest pirate treasures ever cached along North America's East Coast would sink to the nondescript pond's depths.

At the center of this fabulous treasure tale is Edward Lowe (sometimes spelled Low) who, in his lifetime, used several aliases. British by birth, Lowe arrived in New England with his parents who were among the early waves of colonizers in Massachusetts. Though only eleven years old at the time, Lowe worked the fields and tended to livestock just as well as any grown man. When he was older, Lowe became a businessman and operated a small store in the coastal village of Salem.

At twenty-eight, Lowe married Elizabeth Morgan and built a small frame house on a high cliff overlooking the Atlantic Ocean. Two years later, Elizabeth died from complications arising from a difficult pregnancy. Lowe, inconsolable and overcome with grief, couldn't bear to remain in Massachusetts and booked passage on a trading vessel bound for South America.

While visiting Brazil, Lowe fell in with pirates and was involved in several raids. Casting off all semblance of a New England businessman, Lowe reveled in the adventure and profit of piracy, and within a few years, he was commanding his own fleet of vessels that sailed both sides of the Atlantic Ocean preying on merchant ships.

In 1723, Lowe heard about the promise of plunder along the New England coast. He decided to abandon the South Atlantic waters and sail northward. Months later, Lowe and his fearsome company of brigands were terrorizing the shores and coastal seas of New England and the Middle-Atlantic.

About the same time Lowe was plundering ships and shoreline communities along the coast, a Spanish pirate vessel escaping a fleet of British warships arrived at Cape Hatteras off the North Carolina shore. Turning northward, the Spanish vessel, the *Don Pedro del Monclava*, managed to stay just ahead of its pursuers for several days, finally eluding the British near Massachusetts. Continuing northward and keeping close to the New Hampshire and Maine shores, the Spanish pirate ship finally took refuge in Casco Bay. After setting anchor in the bay, the Spanish captain sent several members of his crew onto land to procure fresh water and meat while the ship was being readied for another voyage.

For nearly a week, the *Don Pedro* lay at anchor in Casco Bay. When all of the water barrels and meat lockers had finally been filled, the captain gave orders to weigh anchor and set sail.

Just as the *Don Pedro* was leaving Casco Bay, Edward Lowe, in command of a pirate fleet of five ships arrived from the east. Spotting the Spanish vessel, Lowe gave chase.

Minutes later, Lowe's ships overtook the ship and a brief battle ensued. The Spanish leader, realizing he was heavily outnumbered and outgunned, eventually surrendered.

At first, the Spanish captain was uncooperative, but after Lowe subjected him to several hours of horrible torture, he admitted to transporting a large treasure in the hold.

Searching below decks, Lowe and several of his crewmen found the treasure—a large, heavy, wooden chest heaped with gold coins, a myriad of glistening jewels, and three stout nail kegs packed with thin, eighteen-inch-long silver bars. With considerable difficulty, ten men lifted the chest, removed it from the *Don Pedro*, and placed it aboard Lowe's ship.

After releasing the Spanish ship, Lowe and his pirates planned to set sail southward when the crew spotted three British warships approaching from the south. Not wishing to be caught with the gold, silver, and jewels that had just been taken from the Spaniards, Lowe ordered his ships toward the closest island where he intended to hide the treasure.

Quickly anchoring just off Pond Island, Lowe, with the help of several crewmen in three rowboats, transported the treasure from the ship to the island. As quickly as possible, the sailors carried and dragged the heavy booty to the pond and pushed it in. Just as the last of the gold and silver vanished beneath the pond's waters, the British ships opened fire on Lowe's fleet.

After returning to his vessel, Lowe directed a spirited defense against the attacking British, but after one of his ships sank from heavy cannon fire, it became apparent to the pirate leader that the British ships possessed superior armament. Rather than remain and fight, Lowe chose instead to attempt an escape, and, setting sail, he directed his boats around the attackers and fled to the open sea. For a week, the British pursued Lowe, but eventually they fell back and abandoned the chase altogether.

Fearful of remaining in North American waters, Lowe sailed for the Caribbean. He would return, he decided, in a few years when British warships had vacated the region.

Lowe did not fare well in the Caribbean. On one occasion, his ships attacked a merchant vessel and the pirates discovered too late that they were completely outgunned and were repelled. In another incident, Lowe attacked a French ship, but it sank two of the pirate's three-masters with well-placed cannon fire. Lowe, again outgunned and outmaneuvered, attempted to escape, but was overtaken by the French ship and captured. After a brief trial, Lowe, along with his surviving crew members, was convicted of piracy and hanged.

Neither Lowe nor any of the pirates involved in hiding the great treasure on Pond Island lived to return to Casco Bay, and for decades only a few who heard the confession of one of Lowe's aides knew about the existence of the buried cache.

This little-known treasure has not been actively searched for until recent years when several men, using sensing equipment, scanned Pond Island's relatively small body of water. Initially, the results were negative, but it was later learned that the pond had an extremely soft bottom. It is now suspected by some that Lowe's huge treasure chest of riches sank to an undetermined depth in the mud because of their enormous weight.

Every reason exists that Lowe's fortune still lies in the pond, but it will take a sophisticated and expensive retrieval operation to recover it.

NEW HAMPSHIRE

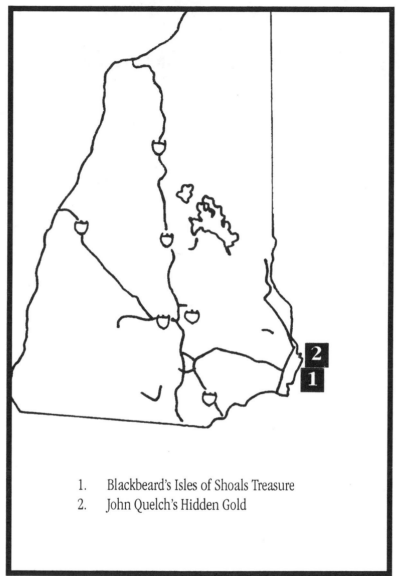

Blackbeard's Isles of Shoals Treasure

A few miles out in the Atlantic Ocean, just off the New Hampshire shore, rests a cluster of nine small islands. Named the Isles of Shoals, these mostly bare rock protrusions have been visited by pirates since the early 1700s. Among the many brigands believed to have stashed treasure there is the notorious Blackbeard himself, one of the most feared freebooters in history, especially in the waters of the Atlantic and Caribbean.

Blackbeard, who often went by the name Edward Teach, first visited the Isles of Shoals around 1710. After exploring each of them, he determined the islands would be ideal for hiding because they were remote, unpopulated, and had few safe harbors. Blackbeard occasionally visited the islands from time to time, but it wasn't until 1715 that he buried a large treasure on White Island, the southernmost isle of this tiny archipelago.

Blackbeard came into the first treasure that he buried on White Island because of a chance encounter with a man known only as Scott. Early in 1715, Blackbeard commanded a pirate vessel along the west coast of Scotland when he decided to drop anchor in Glasgow Bay. That evening, a rowboat was spotted approaching the pirate ship, and, with dozens of weapons pointed at him, the single oarsman tied up his vessel to the ship, climbed aboard, and requested a meeting with Blackbeard. For several hours, the pirate leader and the newcomer engaged in secret conversation in Blackbeard's cabin. When they finally exited, the stranger was introduced to the crew as Captain Scott, a man who possessed important information about a merchant vessel transporting gold ingots and coins.

Early the next morning, the pirate ship lifted anchor, sailed out of the bay, and proceeded southward along the coast. Two days later, the merchant ship was encountered. Following an intense battle in which dozens of men on both ships were killed, Blackbeard's forces prevailed and the vessel was captured. For two days, Blackbeard and Scott directed the loading of the treasure and goods into the hold of the pirate vessel.

Placing Scott in command of the captured ship, Blackbeard and his new ally then sailed along the French and Spanish coasts, plundering ships and stealing treasure along the way.

Weeks later, the two ships returned to Glasgow, and Scott was rowed to shore. The following day, he returned with a young woman he said was his mistress. After two days of replenishing supplies and making certain the ships were completely seaworthy, Blackbeard and Scott set sail for the open Atlantic and weeks later landed just offshore of White Island. After nearly an entire week, Blackbeard's sailors transported all the treasure taken from the recent raids to the small island and buried it in a secret location.

Building materials were shipped from the nearby New Hampshire shore to White Island, and a cabin was constructed for Scott and his mistress. When Blackbeard returned to the sea and piracy a few weeks later, Scott and the woman remained on the island to guard the treasure.

On subsequent visits to the Isles of Shoals over the next three years, Blackbeard deposited even more treasure taken in raids on merchant ships, all of it added to the incredible store already there, until the sizeable hoard contained gold and silver ingots and coins, diamonds and rare emeralds, and a great quantity of finely crafted jewelry. Even at that time, it was estimated that the growing pirate hoard was worth several million dollars.

Around 1718, the British government ordered a fleet of warships into the Atlantic Ocean with the express purpose of eliminating piracy. The principal objective was to locate Blackbeard's hideout in the hope of capturing the notorious freebooter. While anchored just off Nova Scotia, the British fleet's commander learned of Blackbeard's hideout on the Isles of Shoals and immediately set out to find him.

As the British warships approached the Isles of Shoals from the northeast, they were spotted by one of Blackbeard's many White Island sentries, and a warning was immediately sent to the pirate leader. Always in a state of readiness, Blackbeard took less than two hours to assemble his crew, board the ship, and set sail. By the time the British vessels reached the Isles of Shoals, Blackbeard had long since escaped and vanished down the Atlantic Coast.

When warned of the approaching ships, Scott was undecided as to whether to flee White Island or remain and take his chances. Finally, he decided it was in his best interest to escape, fearing he would be captured and returned to Scotland for hanging. After ordering his crew aboard ship, he told his young mistress to remain on the island to guard the treasure and made her take an oath she would never reveal where it was buried.

Unfortunately, Scott waited too long to make his decision to leave the island. By the time the sails were raised on his ship, the British warships appeared and immediately attacked. A fierce battle erupted and more than a hundred cannonballs were fired. Scott's vessel exploded into flames and sank. Only a few crewmen managed to swim ashore, but Scott was not among them. Stranded and with no one to provide for her, Scott's mistress, unable to leave the island, eventually starved to death.

Months later when apprised of the death of Scott and his mistress, Blackbeard said that there was now no one left alive except for himself who knew the secret location of his great treasure buried on White Island.

Blackbeard never returned to the Isles of Shoals. American warships eventually cornered him in Okracoke Inlet off the North Carolina shore and during a protracted battle killed the pirate.

Years later when the existence of Blackbeard's buried treasure on the Isles of Shoals became commonplace, treasure hunters went to White Island in search of it. The quest continues today, since the treasure cache has never been discovered.

In the nearly three hundred years since the trove's burial, no evidence of an excavation would be apparent today. Armies of metal detector-toting treasure hunters have combed White Island during the past few decades, but only an occasional gold coin or artifact has been located.

And for good reason, Blackbeard allegedly buried his treasure sixty feet beneath the Isles of Shoals sands!

John Quelch's Hidden Gold

John Quelch, unlike his pirate counterparts, did not strike up fear on the high seas. In fact, Quelch was relatively unknown in pirate circles and actually served most of his seafaring career as a crew member of a well-armed private ship commissioned by the British government. So for years, Quelch hunted and eliminated the pirate menace that plagued the Atlantic shores. But his career changed in the 1720s when one day, the privateer encountered a Spanish pirate ship off the Florida coast and gave pursuit.

A two-hour battle ensued during which the privateer continuously shelled the pirate vessel with long distance cannon fire. The Spanish ship finally sank in very shallow water only about two hundred yards from shore. Convinced the pirate ship was transporting a fortune in stolen treasure, Quelch's commander ordered the sailors to dive to the wreck and retrieve the loot.

For several days, Quelch and his fellow seamen removed hundreds of gold ingots from the sunken vessel and loaded them into the privateer.

For weeks afterward, Quelch remained intrigued with the amount of gold he and the others retrieved from the Spanish ship, and this interest strongly remained with him for the rest of his life. Quelch gradually realized that piracy paid considerably better than working on a privateer. With visions of easily attainable riches, Quelch arranged several clandestine meetings with two dozen of the ship's sailors, and soon the group began to formulate plans to take over the vessel.

One morning about two weeks later, as the unsuspecting privateer's captain was leaving his cabin, he was attacked, subdued, bound tightly with sail cord, and locked in the galley. At the first opportunity, he was placed in a rowboat and transported to shore. Once rid of the captain, the ship, now under Quelch's command, sailed away.

Several weeks later, Quelch and his crew of ambitious pirates arrived just off the coast of Spain, and for the next few months plied the coastal waters of western Europe and Africa, preying on Spanish and Portuguese merchant vessels. Finally, with his ship laboring under the incredible weight of thousands of pounds of captured gold and other treasures, Quelch recrossed the Atlantic to the American shore where he intended to search for a suitable location to bury his wealth.

During his piracy activities, Quelch grew more and more obsessed with gold—ingots, coins, nuggets, dust, and jewelry. The color, the texture, even the taste of gold was like a narcotic to Quelch, and he worried that he would never obtain enough of the metal to satisfy himself. All other treasures that were stolen were divided among the other pirates, but Quelch always maintained possession of any gold.

After sailing up and down the east coast of America for several weeks, Quelch finally decided on Star Island in the Isles of Shoals as the most suitable location for caching his treasure. At a secret location on the island, Quelch ordered several deep holes excavated, and into each he placed portions of his great fortune. Estimates of Quelch's cache ranged from one hundred thousand to several million.

During subsequent years, Quelch ranged across the Atlantic on at least three more occasions acquiring booty, which he added to his Star Island cache. Once, after a particularly harrowing expedition during which he intended to raid several American coastal villages, he was nearly captured by American warships. Deciding he'd had enough of piracy, Quelch turned the boat over to his crew and returned to Star Island for good.

Though Quelch was no longer interested in piracy, the Americans still considered him a dangerous criminal, and when his Star Island hiding place became known to officials, a small fleet of warships commanded by Major Sewell and Captain John Turner was sent to the Isles of Shoals to capture the ex-brigand.

Utterly defenseless and taken completely by surprise, Quelch surrendered to the Americans. When asked where he had hidden all of his gold, he remained silent, and a search of his cabin yielded only a small sack of gold coins and nuggets. Quelch concealed his treasure so well that a subsequent organized search of the island found no evidence of a cache.

Quelch was tried for piracy and sentenced to prison for life. He never returned to Star Island and eventually died from consumption.

Throughout his pirate career, Quelch managed to keep a low profile and was known by very few. Other than a limited number of officials and commanders of warships that pursued Quelch, few were aware of his fortune in stolen treasure.

Nearly sixty years after Quelch's death in prison, an old, tattered journal was discovered in a locked wooden trunk found in the attic of a vacant house near Glouchester, Massachusetts. The journal, believed to have been written by Quelch, told of an incredible fortune in gold ingots and coins buried somewhere on Star Island. Unfortunately, no directions were provided relative to the location of the secret cache.

The discovery of the journal generated a great deal of interest among area treasure hunters, and for many years, boats would arrive on the shores of Star Island carrying searchers who explored up and down the shores and across the bare rock seeking some evidence of a hiding place, but they always came away empty-handed.

During the last decade of the 1700s, workers were building a seawall around a portion of Star Island using the native stones found on the island. While gathering some stones near the western end, one worker uncovered several gold ingots. The discovery stimulated another series of searches by treasure hunters, but, save for the initial discovery, nothing else was ever found.

Months before he was captured, John Quelch expressed to one of his crewmen the fear that people would someday come to Star Island to take his treasure away. Therefore, he said, he intended to hide it so well that no one would ever find it.

It appears that pirate Quelch was, indeed, successful.

MASSACHUSETTS

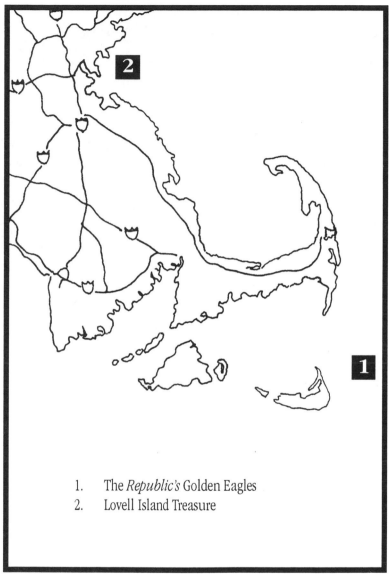

The *Republic's* Golden Eagles

On the cold and foggy morning of January 22, 1909, the *S.S. Republic* left the port of New York. Along with nearly four hundred twenty passengers bound for a winter cruise in the Mediterranean Sea, the ship transported a cargo of food stores for a naval fleet stationed off Gibraltar and relief supplies for earthquake victims in Italy. Several kegs of ten-dollar gold pieces called golden eagles were also stored in a large metal safe. The fifteen-ton ship boasted twin screws, four masts, a single funnel, and an iron hull capable of a top speed of seventeen knots per hour.

As Captain Sealby stood in the pilothouse on the first day of the transatlantic voyage, he watched the prow of the great ship cut through the dense, swirling fog. Peering into the dimness, Sealby could not shake a growing uneasy feeling, a premonition that something bad was going to happen. He tried to crowd the strange sensation aside by busying himself with various duties as the ship paralleled the coast toward Nantucket Island, but it continued to nag him.

At Nantucket, the *S.S. Republic* struck an eastward course across the Atlantic, the normal route for outgoing ships. Because of the fog, however, the ship made slow progress.

On the evening of the twenty-third, the *S.S. Republic* was only about thirty miles east of the Massachusetts coast when Captain Sealby's fear of disaster suddenly grew stronger. Uncomfortable with navigating through the heavy fog, Sealby was about to confess his feelings of imminent danger to his aide when he heard a watchman screaming that there was a ship bearing down on them off the starboard bow.

Meanwhile, the captain and crew of the Italian liner *Florida* were also experiencing difficulty with the weather. The New York-bound ship, overloaded with nine hundred passengers, was traveling at fifteen knots when it was spotted by the bow watch of the *S.S. Republic*. Hours earlier, the *Florida* had become lost in the North Atlantic, and was now about thirty miles off the normal course.

Seconds after Sealby heard the warning from the watch, the *Florida* rammed into the side of the *Republic*, sending its bow almost halfway through the American ship and killing two of its crewmen. Four *Florida* crewmen also died in the collision.

S.S. Republic wireless operator Jack Binns, a veteran of forty Atlantic crossings, immediately sent out a distress call, providing latitude and longitude of the accident. Sealby ran from the pilothouse to inspect the damage and was stunned to discover both engine rooms were filled with sea water. After being reassured that his entire engine crew had survived the collision and escaped to the upper deck, Sealby ordered several of his sailors to begin alerting the passengers to prepare to board lifeboats. As this task was being carried out, Sealby started giving some thought to offloading the kegs of golden eagles onto the *Florida* when he was distracted by a series of collision-related emergencies.

The two huge ships foundered in the sea, locked together in a disastrous tangle. Passengers and crew from both vessels began milling around on the decks in confusion. Many of the *S.S. Republic*'s passengers, fearful that the ship was going to sink and unable to find a lifeboat station, began scrambling onto the deck of the *Florida*. Several nearby vessels began responding to the distress signal, including four Coast Guard cutters. The worsening fog, however, delayed rescue efforts and caused two of the cutters to become lost.

The *Florida*'s captain had a knotty dilemma—to leave his ship embedded in the *Republic* and risk the sinking of both vessels, or to withdraw and hasten the American ship's descent to the bottom. After conferring with his crew and Captain Sealby, the captain of the *Florida* ordered the engines reversed only after all of the passengers of the *Republic* had been transferred or placed in lifeboats. Only Captain Sealby and twenty-nine crew members remained on board.

After pulling free from the *Republic*, the *Florida* remained at the side of the American vessel until the Coast Guard cutters arrived and towed it to shore. Within a short time, three other ships—the *Baltic*, the *Lorraine*, and the *Lucania*, sailed into view and hovered nearby in case they were needed.

Within an hour, a stiff wind blew in from the east and much of the fog dissipated. Two Coast Guard cutters soon arrived and attached twelve-inch hawsers to the *Republic* and began towing it back toward New York. Sealby feared the *Republic* would not remain afloat long enough to reach safety, but he hoped it would at least get towed to relatively shallow waters so that, should it sink, the golden eagles could be easily retrieved.

As the cutters slowly pulled the *Republic* toward the coast, water flowed into the damaged ship at an increasing rate. Finally, Sealby ordered his crew into lifeboats and informed the two cutters' skippers to cut the hawsers.

Only minutes after Sealby and the last of his crew members rowed away in a lifeboat, the *Republic* briefly tilted bow-upward and then quickly sank two hundred forty feet to the ocean's bottom, twenty miles east of Nantucket Island. Miraculously, only two of the five hundred passengers and crewmen aboard were killed, but millions of dollars worth of United States ten-dollar golden eagles went down with the S.S. *Republic*.

In 1919, a Chicago-based salvage and recovery organization examined the possibility of recovering the gold coins, but the great depth of the wreck rendered the operation unsafe.

For nearly two decades, the *Republic* rested undisturbed on the continental shelf just over twenty miles from the Massachusetts shore. Between 1919 and 1927, three more salvage operators examined the possibilities of recovering the kegs of gold coins, but, with the poor state of diving gear at the time, the trio decided the undertaking was too dangerous.

In 1928, a salvage company from England, learned of the three million dollars' worth of golden eagles lying in the *Republic*'s hulk and decided to attempt a recovery. The divers, wearing heavy, clumsy diving suits, managed to reach the *Republic* and reported that it rested on one side. Using underwater torches, they cut away a portion of the hull in order to reach the chamber that contained the safe filled with kegs of gold coins, but they were confronted with a web-like network of twisted steel girders and plates that made entry impossible. Between this formidable obstacle and the ever-present danger of sharks, the British salvage team packed up and left.

In 1963, noted Michigan salvor L.B. Copeman held a news conference and claimed he knew a way to retrieve the treasure. As he was making preparations to journey to the Atlantic, however, he suffered a severe heart attack and died.

Since Copeman, at least two other salvage companies have attempted to retrieve the golden eagles, but they encountered the same obstacles as the British team.

The continental shelf location of the *Republic*'s sunken hulk is well known to treasure hunters; it even appears on some coastal water maps. The golden eagles, still lying in the wreckage two hundred forty feet below the surface, would be worth several times more than their original three million dollar value today. They continue to provide a temptation to those attracted to the tragic story of the *Republic*.

The brave soul who can solve the dilemma of deep water, sharks, and, most importantly, conquering the dangerous maze of twisted steel, will become a millionaire many times over.

Lovell Island Treasure

Ships always had a hard time maneuvering to Lovell Island, a small area of land in the mouth of Boston Harbor. Located between the Deer Island peninsula to the northwest and the Nantasket peninsula to the southeast, Lovell Island, barely has an elevation above sea level. Until a lighthouse was built, many a ship captain wrecked his vessel on the island named for the early Massachusetts pioneer William Lovell. This collision course has left a wealth of pirate booty on this island's coast.

In 1782, a French flotilla under the command of the noted seaman Admiral Vaubaird was entering Boston Harbor when disaster struck. Commanded by Captain David Darling, the lead ship, the *Magnifique*, was transporting a huge fortune in gold and silver coins. The money formed the foundation of a French treasury to be established in America that would provide payment to soldiers for the procurement of needed supplies. Estimates of the worth of the kegs and chests of coins carried in the *Magnifique*'s hold has ranged from $350,000 to more than $4 million.

The *Magnifique* was on a collision course with Lovell Island before Captain Darling became aware it lay in the path of the vessel. Only seconds after the bow watchman screamed a warning, the *Magnifique* slammed into the island, shattering several timbers along the starboard side and killing three crewmen.

Admiral Vaubaird commanded Darling to guide the fleet into Boston Harbor on the basis of his oft-repeated claim that he was well acquainted with the area's waters. If Darling was ever aware of Lovell Island's existence, he had apparently forgotten it. The wrecked *Magnifique* quickly filled with water, listed dramatically to one side, and sank. Admiral Vaubaird ordered several seamen to dive to the wreck and try to retrieve the coins, but they were unsuccessful. After three days, Vaubaird abandoned the salvage attempt.

Darling was dismissed from Vaubaird's command and spent much of the remainder of his life enduring taunts and ridicule because of his inept seamanship.

For a time, portions of the *Magnifique* protruded above the sea's surface, but as weeks passed and storms raged across the area, the churning waters carried the wrecked ship some distance south of the island where it finally came to rest at the bottom of the harbor.

Over the years, a few who were aware of the *Magnifique* and of its great treasure's existence, tried to locate it, intending to recover the coins. Unfortunately for the treasure seekers, the shifting sands of the sea floor bottom alternately covered and uncovered the wreck. During the summer of 1859, a salvage team exploring the waters just south of Lovell Island brought up several rotten timbers believed to be from the *Magnifique*, but little else was found. Subsequent underwater retrieval attempts fared no better.

Because of Lovell Island's dangerous position in Boston Harbor, a lighthouse was eventually constructed to warn approaching ships. During the 1920s, the lighthouse keeper, Charles Jennings, spent his time exploring the beaches of the island when he wasn't tending to the lighthouse. One afternoon as he dug in the sand on one of the southern beaches, he uncovered a flat, round object coated with a thick layer of corrosion. As he continued to dig, Jennings found nearly a dozen more.

Taking them home, Jennings cleaned the coating from the strange pieces and was surprised to discover they were gold and silver coins of French mint, all dated before 1782. Knowing a bit of history connected to the *Magnifique*, Jennings was certain he had found some of the treasure, which apparently had washed up on the shore. Subsequent excavations during the following weeks yielded approximately fifty more coins.

About two months after finding the first coins, Jennings left Lovell Island for a week to visit relatives on the mainland. While he was gone, a substitute lighthouse keeper, Stewart Frasier, was appointed to take his place. While briefing Frasier on the maintenance of the lighthouse, Jennings mentioned finding the French coins on the beach, even describing the exact locations of the discoveries.

It proved to be a mistake. When Jennings returned from his trip, he found the lighthouse abandoned and Frasier gone. During a walk along the beach, Jennings noted several deep holes dug in the area where he initially found the coins.

Weeks later, Jennings learned from a relative that Frasier, having suddenly and mysteriously come into a fortune, had recently moved from Boston to Virginia where he was in the process of building a fine new home. Jennings was convinced Frasier found more of the French gold and silver coins, enough to make him wealthy. During the next few years, Jennings continued to search the beaches for coins, eventually finding another two hundred.

Researchers believe all of the available evidence points to the notion that Jennings and Frasier found coins from the wreck of the *Magnifique*. Many of the coins, freed from their rotting chests and kegs through the years, washed up on the Lovell Island shore during violent storms. Researchers are also convinced that Jennings' and Frasier's discoveries represent only a tiny fraction of the treasure transported by the *Magnifique* and that, given today's gold and silver values, millions of dollars' worth of the fortune still lie scattered between the sunken French ship's remains and the shore.

In recent years, beachcombers and treasure hunters equipped with sensitive electronic detectors have discovered dozens more French coins on Lovell Island's south shore.

Beyond the shore and extending hundreds of yards into the waters of the harbor, it is probable that millions of dollars'worth of the gold and silver coins still lie strewn in the bottom sands.

RHODE ISLAND

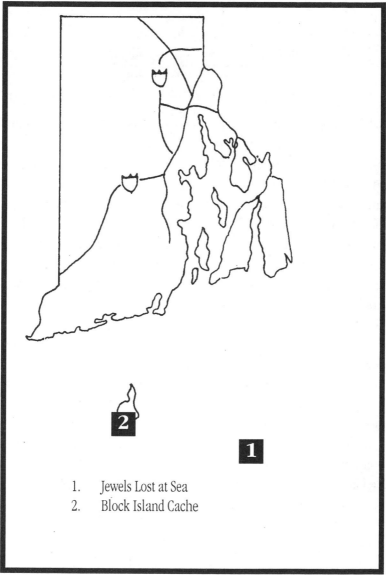

1. Jewels Lost at Sea
2. Block Island Cache

Jewels Lost at Sea

In 1864, approximately forty miles southeast of the Rhode Island shore, a Russian steamer, transporting South American emeralds valued at $3 million, sank 250 feet. Despite dozens of attempts to locate it, the wreck of the *Spasskaya* has never been found, and among the rotten timbers and rusted machinery lying at the bottom of the Atlantic Ocean, a fortune remains in Columbian emeralds awaiting the patient and fortunate treasure hunter.

During the Civil War, one of the few foreign powers maintaining friendly relations with the United States government was Russia. As a result of comparable and compatible philosophies regarding trade and trade routes, United States President Abraham Lincoln and Russian Tsar Alexander II often exchanged ideas and plans to expand trade and shipping opportunities. However, the British and French were antagonistic toward the Americans, the Russians, and their growing Atlantic commerce and often sent warships to disrupt trade and shipping.

In December 1863, the Russian steamer *Spasskaya*, following a long voyage across the Baltic Sea and Atlantic Ocean, docked at the Caribbean port of Cartagena, Columbia. Like the Americans, the Columbians sought friendly trade relations with the Russians, and the arrival of the *Spasskaya* was cause for celebration. While the Cartagena officials entertained the captain and crew of the Russian vessel, the city streets jammed with revelers.

The Columbians were so highly committed to cultivating trade relations with the Russians that they presented a gift to Tsar

Alexander II: a fine wooden chest filled with uncut emeralds from the country's richest mine. On the morning following the festivities, the chest bearing the emeralds was carried aboard the *Spasskaya* and secured below deck. Three weeks later, the steamer sailed out of port for Russia, its hold filled with Columbian cargo and a fortune in emeralds.

After crossing the Caribbean Sea and arriving off the Florida coast, the *Spasskaya* paralleled the American shoreline for several days, arriving finally at the port of New York. Because of the good relations between the two nations, Russian vessels were always welcome in American ports. In New York, the ship's captain met with Union officials and reaffirmed Russia's political support. For two weeks, the Russians remained in port while the crew replenished the ship's supplies. With preparations completed, the Russians sailed out of the harbor and commenced their long journey home.

As the *Spasskaya* passed out of the harbor and sailed along Long Island's southern shore, residents stood on the beaches to observe the unique ship. The *Spasskaya* was unlike most cargo vessels that sailed Atlantic waters. In addition to a three-masted set of sails, the ship boasted two large paddle wheels mounted on each side of the hull. The funnels carrying the exhaust from the engines lay horizontal along the length of the deck to keep sparks from setting fire to the canvas rigging.

The *Spasskaya* departed the New York harbor under sail. After passing the eastern end of Long Island, the Russians encountered a violent winter storm moving in from the Atlantic Ocean, and the captain immediately ordered the sails lowered. Certain that the gale would be short-lived, he ordered the engines fired up and the ship to proceed along the established course. As the *Spasskaya* passed out of the southern limit of Rhode Island Sound and into the open ocean, the storm increased in fury. Before the ship could be turned back toward shore, powerful and savage winds in excess of forty knots whipped across the surface generating twenty-foot waves that punished the *Spasskaya*, hurling and bouncing it across the waters.

A proven seaworthy vessel, the *Spasskaya* was not constructed to endure such an intense storm. With timbers torn and weakened from the battering along with the vicious hammering of the extremely high waves, the ship soon took on water at a frightening rate. Suddenly, a huge wave smashed into the vessel and capsized it. The *Spasskaya*, along with the entire crew and cargo, quickly plunged to the bottom.

With no eyewitnesses, historians are not entirely certain where the *Spasskaya* went down. A general area covering several square miles of ocean southeast of the Rhode Island coast has been searched for more than one hundred years, but no sign of the *Spasskaya*'s wreckage has ever been found. While dozens of wrecks in this region have been located and identified, the treasure-laden Russian vessel has eluded searchers.

Along with the *Spasskaya*, the incredible fortune in uncut emeralds, remains lost today. However, they still lure treasure hunters from around the world who travel to this coastal area searching for the jewels that never reached their intended destination.

Block Island Cache

Block Island is a prominent isle about twelve miles south of the Rhode Island shore and separated from the mainland by Block Island Sound. Because it could be easily defended, the island was a popular hideout for pirates and other outlaws during the late 1600s. Although numerous noted Atlantic pirates frequented Block Island, only British freebooter Joseph Bradish is known to have actually buried treasure there.

The pirate Bradish (sometimes spelled Braddish), commanding a three-masted vessel named the *Adventure*, arrived late one spring off the New England shore following several raids of Spanish ships in the Caribbean Sea. With a hold filled with gold and jewelry taken from the Spaniards, Bradish intended to invade small settlements located along the Atlantic Coast from Massachusetts to South Carolina until reaching the port of Charleston. At Charleston, Bradish intended to unload the treasure, pay off his crew, send them on their way, and sell the ship. Then, Bradish planned to retire from piracy forever and settle into a comfortable living in this growing city.

During the Caribbean raids, however, the *Adventure* suffered severe damage to one side of the hull, and by the time the ship reached the American coast, it was evident that repairs would have to be made soon. Having used Block Island many times in the past as a retreat and sanctuary, Bradish now navigated his injured ship to that small island.

After inspecting the damage to the *Adventure*, Bradish deter-mined the vessel needed some new planking and metal fittings. He organized a crew of six men to row a longboat the short distance to Newport, Rhode Island, and make arrangements for purchase and delivery of the materials.

Unknown to Bradish, most of the area's coastal communities had suffered several recent pirate depredations and were on the defensive. When Bradish's crew arrived at Newport, they were immediately recognized as pirates and arrested. Under question-ing, the pirates revealed their leader's identity and admitted that he, along with thirty crewmen, were encamped on Block Island.

After waiting three days for his crew members to return, Bradish grew increasingly concerned. On the morning of the fourth day, he was convinced his sailors had been identified as pirates and were being detained. The pirate leader knew it was now only a matter of time before authorities learned of his presence on Block Island. Expecting a raid at any moment, Bradish had his chests of gold coins and jewels unloaded from the *Adventure* and carried to a spot on the southern beach of the island. There, several holes were dug and the treasure was lowered into them. While the chests were being buried, Bradish noted a nearby stunted oak tree growing out of a crevice in a section of exposed bedrock. This tree, thought Bradish, would mark the cache's location.

Bradish eventually received word that his men had been cap-tured and that coastal residents were planning to raid Block Island. The pirate menace was to be eliminated once and for all! Armed citizens gathered from several miles away to join in the assault. In an attempt to deceive the authorities, Bradish had the *Adventure* scuttled and sunk to look as if Block Island had been abandoned.

For two days, the island-bound pirates awaited the attack. On the evening of the second day, a scout arrived with information that a force of nearly four hundred armed men were gathered at Point Judith and were preparing to row out to Block Island in the morning. Realizing his sailors could not defend themselves against such a large force, Bradish ordered the hasty construction of several crude rafts from the *Adventure*'s remains. Once the rafts were completed, the pirates left the island under cover of night and floated to the Rhode Island mainland, landing near the present-day town of Weekapaug. Bradish intended to remain there in hiding until it was convenient and safe to steal a ship. Once a suitable vessel was obtained, he would sail to Block Island, retrieve the treasure, and flee down the coast. For several days, the pirates remained hidden, but eventually their food supply was exhausted. When Bradish and five sailors attempted to walk to a nearby settlement to try to obtain supplies, they were spotted and apprehended.

While Bradish was being held in the jail at Newport, authorities learned the British government was offering a large reward for the pirate. After alerting the British of Bradish's capture, the pirate was manacled hand and foot, placed aboard a ship, and returned to England. In London, Bradish was tried and found guilty of several charges of piracy and hanged in 1700.

Just before his execution, Bradish tried to purchase his freedom. Calling two prison guards close, he told them about his great treasure cached on Block Island. If they released him, he whispered, he would take them to the secret location near the stunted oak tree, dig up the gold and jewels, and split the fortune with them. The guards agreed to participate in the scheme but were foiled by a companion who was upset about not being included. One week later, Bradish was hanged.

Back in the United States, one of the pirates who helped Bradish bury his treasure was finally released from prison in 1721 after serving twenty years of hard labor. Convinced the gold and jewels he helped bury were still on Block Island, he decided to return to the location, retrieve the fortune, and purchase passage to South America.

The former pirate rented a skiff and rowed out to the southern end of Block Island. Rowing past several fishermen in the sound, he finally landed on the shore he believed to be the one where the treasure was buried. Remembering a nearby stunted oak tree, the ex-pirate searched for it but to no avail. He walked around the area from the waterline to the exposed rock above the beach but found nothing at all familiar about the landscape. Thinking he might have landed on the wrong beach, he tried several more, all with the same results. Finally, after spending four days on the island, he returned to the mainland and was never seen again.

Others have come to Block Island in search of the lost Bradish cache. Virginian Winston Lockhart arrived in Providence in 1872, carrying a parchment map he claimed was given to him by a descendant of one of Bradish's crewmen. The map clearly portrayed the irregular Rhode Island coastline and Block Island just to the south. On the southern shore of Block Island was an "X" with an accompanying legend stating "treasure buried here." A picture of a stunted tree was drawn near the "X."

After Lockhart arrived at the location marked on the map, he immediately undertook a search for the stunted tree. Unlike the former crewman who searched for the cache, and much to his dismay, Lockhart found dozens of such trees. After excavating hundreds of holes next to most of the trees, Lockhart finally gave up his search and returned to Virginia. The map seems to have disappeared with time.

In 1964, two men were camped on the southern shore of Block Island while fishing in the waters of the sound. Preparing breakfast over an open fire one morning, one of the men discovered three gold coins in the sand near where he sat. He later showed the coins to friends on the mainland, who told him the story of Bradish's loot for the first time. They suggested to him that the coins might be part of the treasure. A week later, accompanied by three boatloads of friends and relatives, the two men returned to Block Island. Once there, however, they became uncertain where the exact location of their campsite had been. Nothing was ever found.

In 1978, Providence automobile mechanic Mark Kennedy was hiking a portion of Block Island during a free weekend when he discovered a wooden chest partially uncovered in the sands of a beach at the island's southern end. Assuming the chest belonged to someone nearby, Kennedy walked on. When he related the discovery several days later, he, like others before him, was told about Bradish's treasure. On a return trip to the island, however, Kennedy was unable to locate the chest.

Since the time Bradish originally cached his treasure, storm winds and strong tidal surges have deposited heavy loads of sediment across Block Island. Other times, nature effectively erodes and simply carries the sand away. It is likely that Bradish's treasure cache has been exposed and later covered several times since its original burial. Some day, perhaps, someone will be exploring the southern beaches of Block Island following a severe storm that has removed some of the beach sand. He may stumble luckily upon chests packed with pirate Bradish's lost coins and jewels.

CONNECTICUT

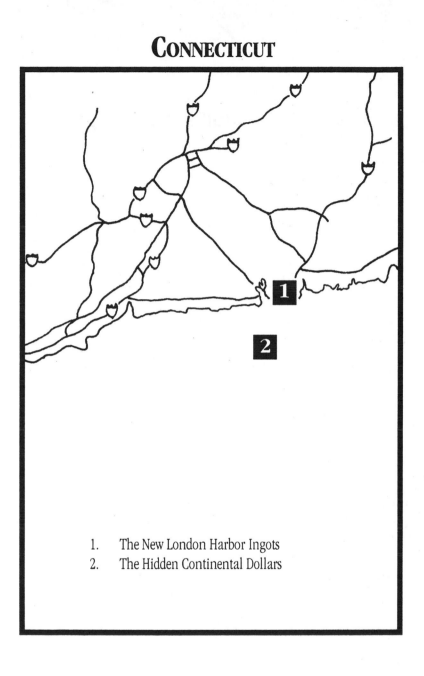

The New London Harbor Ingots

Four wooden chests containing gold and silver ingots lie some-where on the bottom of the New London Harbor. The treasure's depth is unknown, but is presumed to be near an old wooden dock used during the 1750s. The treasure was originally part of a precious cargo *en route* to Spain, but a series of emergencies and bizarre events caused it to be sidetracked to this Atlantic coastal location and subsequently to disappear in the bay.

The treasure, consisting of hundreds of eighteen-inch long gold and silver ingots, was packed into forty-one wooden chests rein-forced with metal bands and loaded onto the Spanish galleon *Santa Elena y San Jose* while it was docked at Tampico, a Mexican port. The ingots represented only a small percentage of a great quantity of gold and silver dug with Indian slave labor from several rich mines in the Sierra Madres of western Mexico. The bullion was scheduled to be transported to Spain where it would be added to that country's growing treasury. Then, these finances would be used to purchase arms and materials for the expansion of Spanish influence around the world and to defend the nation against invaders.

Captain Manuel de Urranaga, a competent sailor with a dozen years of service in the Spanish navy and a veteran of at least ten Atlantic crossings, commanded the *San Jose*. After directing the loading of the treasure into the hold of the *San Jose*, Captain Urranaga set sail for Cuba where the Spaniards intended to replenish supplies.

After remaining docked in Cuba for a week, the *San Jose* departed for the long transatlantic journey to Spain. Just south of the Bahama Islands, however, the *San Jose* developed a leak and began taking on water. Concerned, Urranaga decided to return to Cuba, but the mast watch detected a heavy storm developing back to the west and cautioned the captain against sailing into it. Instead, Urranaga turned and headed for the coast of America.

Several miles off the Florida coast, the *San Jose* encountered the American brig *Susannah*, piloted by Captain John Simpson. Urranaga raised a distress flag and the *Susannah* pulled alongside.

Simpson was invited aboard the *San Jose*, and he and Urranaga inspected the leak. The two experienced seamen agreed on the necessity of repair before attempting an Atlantic crossing. While examining the hull, Simpson noted wooden chests lashed to the ship's framework. When he inquired about their contents, Urranaga admitted each contained a fortune in gold and silver ingots.

Once the two officers were topside, Simpson offered to escort the *San Jose* to his home port of New London, Connecticut, and see that the vessel received the necessary repair. Urranaga agreed to the proposition, and soon the two ships were sailing northward to Connecticut.

The *San Jose* and the *Susannah* reached the New London harbor on November 24, 1752. Because of treacherous underwater shoals, Simpson volunteered Daniel Vosper, one of his navigators, to pilot the *San Jose* to the dock. Despite Vosper's navigational skills, he managed to run the Spanish ship onto the rocks. A smaller ship, the *Mary Elizabeth*, commanded by Captain J.L. Gardner, immediately approached the *Susannah* from the New London harbor. Moments after Gardner pulled the *Mary Elizabeth* alongside the American brig, Simpson climbed aboard, then sailed toward the stranded Spanish galleon. When Gardner offered to tow the *San Jose* off the rocks and into the harbor, Urranaga accepted. A short time later, however, Gardner ran the Spanish ship onto another set of shoals.

By this time, yet another ship left the New London harbor and approached the *San Jose*. The owner of this vessel, Andrew McKenzie, offered to unload Urranaga's cargo onto his own ship and see to its safe delivery to the dock. At this point, Lieutenant Jose de San Juan, the officer assigned to handle the cargo, rejected the offer. Pulling Urranaga aside, San Juan told him he believed the Americans were attempting to steal the treasure.

After refusing McKenzie's offer, Urranaga sent the American ships away, and the *San Jose* remained perched precariously upon the rocky shoal. As Urranaga and his crewmen sought a solution to their problems, a dark and heavy storm approached from the south. Within an hour, strong winds and high waves pounded the *San Jose*, battering it against the sharp rocks.

When the violent storm slightly abated, the *Susannah* and a second ship, the *Duquesne,* commanded by Richard Durfey, approached the *San Jose* with offers to transport its cargo to safety. Following some discussion, Urranaga agreed to let Durfey load the gold and silver into the *Duquesne*. Before returning to the dock, ·Urranaga sent San Juan with the cargo to see to its safety. After San Juan sailed away with Durfey, Urranaga agreed to have Simpson employ the *Susannah* to tow the *San Jose* into port.

By dawn of the following day, word had spread through New London that a Spanish vessel was tied up at the dock. Later, the town whirled with news that the local ship *Dusquesne* was carrying millions of dollars' worth of gold and silver taken from the *San Jose*. By mid-morning, approximately three hundred men had gathered on the docks, and the leader of the group announced they intended to attack the *Duquesne* and seize the treasure.

Later in the morning, Gurdon Saltonstall, an assistant to the Connecticut Governor Roger Wolcott, arrived with police force and dispersed the crowd. Saltonstall then informed Urranaga that the *San Jose* treasure needed to be placed under armed guard in a nearby warehouse for safekeeping while the ship was being repaired.

Several laborers, all handpicked by Saltonstall, were assigned to help the Spanish crewmen move the heavy chests. Four workers, however, viewed their new job as an opportunity to steal some of the treasure.

While moving the treasure from the ship's hold to the warehouse, the unwieldy chests had to be carried across the wooden gangplank from the ship to the dock. While moving one of the chests, the four scheming workers, after making certain no one was observing them, dropped it into the bay. Before the entire treasure was removed from the *San Jose*, the quartet of thieves succeeded in depositing a total of four chests into the water. Their plan was to wait until the *San Jose* was finally repaired and on its way to Spain, then slip into the harbor waters in the dark of night and retrieve the booty.

Several weeks passed while the Spaniards, with the help of local craftsmen, worked on repairing the leak in the hull of the *San Jose*. Meanwhile, Urranaga continued to have problems. Captain Durfey assessed a charge of several thousand dollars for transporting the valuable cargo to the dock. Simpson also made a claim for thousands of dollars for towing the *San Jose* to safety. Wrangling over the assessment continued for several weeks, and eventually the claims were taken to court where a judge ordered Urranaga to pay or suffer the seizure of the treasure. The Spaniard, unwilling to part with any portion of his government's treasury, filed numerous appeals. Several months of court deliberations followed, but in the end the initial decision held up and Urranaga was forced to pay.

To compound Urranaga's problems, his crewmen informed him the leak in the *San Jose* could not be repaired. Anxious to leave America, Urranaga arranged for the lease of another ship. When he sought to retrieve the treasure from the warehouse where it was stored, he encountered more difficulties—an exorbitant storage charge had been levied and he was required to obtain the signatures of nearly a dozen officials before receiving permission to remove his own property. Several more months passed before Urranaga finally obtained a release and was allowed to load the treasure into the rented ship.

As the chests were being lowered into the hull, San Juan informed Urranaga that four chests were missing. The captain was so anxious to leave America that he made no mention of the theft to American authorities. Finally, on January 5, 1775, Urranaga sailed out of the New London harbor.

The Spaniards had no sooner disappeared over the eastern horizon of the Atlantic when the four thieves, who had dropped the treasure-filled chests into the bay, began making plans to retrieve them. They obtained ropes and pulleys and planned the recovery for the following night when no one would be on the docks. On this night, however, after the others departed, one of the men returned to the dock and jumped in the cold winter water, straight to the treasure. He intended to remove most of it before dawn and spirit it away before his comrades returned. One of his companions, however, also returned to the dock to undertake his own clandestine recovery. Anger erupted. The two men began shouting, hostile words were exchanged, and one was stabbed to death.

The fight attracted passersby, and the killer was apprehended and taken to jail. During questioning, he confessed to the theft of the Spanish treasure chests and the subsequent plot to steal them for himself. He did not reveal the location of the four chests, but he provided his accomplice's names.

The three men confessed their part in the theft, were tried, found guilty, and sentenced to prison. Two were given twenty-year terms, the murderer life.

During the entire trial, none of the thieves revealed the location of the four missing chests. Alvord Clum, a Newport policeman, visited the men in prison on two occasions and questioned them repeatedly about the treasure. Finally, he persuaded one of them to disclose where the chests were hidden.

After returning to New London, Clum arranged for two divers to explore the area around the dock for the four treasure chests. For two hours, they retraced the harbor bottom but found nothing. Finally, Clum gave up and abandoned the search.

A fellow policeman, Michael Alvin Treadworthy, was intrigued by the case of the missing treasure. Acting on a hunch, he, along with the same two divers, returned to the dock and conducted a second search. As with the previous search, no chests were found, but Treadworthy solved the mystery of their destinies.

The bottom sands of the harbor were very soft, and heavy objects thrown into the water eventually sank to some depth in the loosely consolidated sediment. The heavy trunks, reasoned Treadworthy, simply settled to some indeterminable depth at the very bottom of the bay.

The following day, a score of policemen and volunteers employed long probes trying to locate the chests, but no matter how deep they were plunged into the harbor bottom, they never struck anything solid.

Searchers never recovered the four chests of gold and silver ingots from the New London harbor. They are still there today, resting at some incredible depth near the old wooden dock.

The Hidden Continental Dollars

On the night of November 11, 1779, the *Defense*, a three-masted frigate flying the American flag, bobbed about in the choppy waters of a sheltering cove on the north side of Fisher Island. The worried captain of the ship paced the deck, watchful of the thick storm clouds passing overhead—the dense, moisture-laden layers associated with a squall line that normally precedes a violent storm in these waters. Though the increasing wind and rain concerned the captain, he fretted considerably more about the decision he would have to make.

The weather was not the only thing troubling the *Defense*'s captain. As he peered into the gloomy darkness across the growing whitecaps, he searched for some sign of pursuing warships from the British navy. The captain knew the British were aware the *Defense* was nearby, and it was just a matter of time before the ship was discovered if it remained anchored in the cove. To be overtaken and captured by the British now would subvert the vital mission on which he had been sent. With each passing minute, the captain grew more concerned, for below decks the *Defense* carried five hundred thousand silver coins—Continental one-dollar units packed into several wooden chests. The dollars, each minted from pure silver in 1776, were to be delivered to the young nation's treasury.

The *Defense* also hauled thirty-two cannons and a seasoned crew. The sturdy ship was built low to the water and moved with deceptive speed when all sails were hoisted. Extremely maneuverable, she was adept at avoiding fleets of enemy ships and had done so on several occasions.

As the captain observed the worsening weather, he considered engaging the enemy in a pitched battle rather than having to deal with the oncoming storm.

Finally, and after much deliberation, the captain ordered sails and anchor raised. When the first mate objected to sailing out of the cove and into the advancing storm, the captain responded that if they remained in the cove they would surely be discovered by the British. If the British fleet found them here, capture and death were certainties. With the storm, at least, they had a chance. Furthermore, stated the captain, it was imperative that the silver coins stored in the hull be delivered to the treasury as soon as possible.

Moments later as the sails were hoisted and the strong winds filled the rectangular canvases, the *Defense* moved quickly out of the cove and into Fisher Island Sound. The great weight of the treasure chests in the hold kept the ship dangerously low in the choppy waters, and the captain cringed as they negotiated the open sound. Perhaps, he said to his first mate, they could outrun the storm before it grew much worse and arrive safely at the port of New York.

The moment the *Defense* sailed past the western end of Fisher Island, however, the heavy seas grew stronger. Protected by the sheltered cove where the ship had just sailed, the *Defense*'s captain was unaware of the growing storm's severity. Once the protection of the island was behind them, the surging waves tore at the low-slung boat, crashing over the bows and tearing equipment loose from the deck lashings.

The sky darkened even more, and the captain held tight to a rail as he watched his sailors fight to hold a steady course. At one point, the captain decided to retreat to the shelter of the cove, but the crewmen were unable to turn the ship.

While the captain offered shouts of encouragement to his sailors, the tiller suddenly snapped, and the crew lost all control. Once notified of the rudderless condition, the captain screamed for the sails to be lowered.

It was too late. As the crew rushed to drop the sails, the wind gusts intensified, pushing the out-of-control *Defense* about the waters. The high winds also whipped up towering waves which, at times, swept across the ship's deck carrying men and material into the sea.

For nearly an hour, the *Defense* fought the storm just off Fisher Island Sound's western shore. The high winds cracked all three masts and the hull started breaking apart. The waves grew, pounding the ship without mercy. Pitching about in the rolling, violent seas, the *Defense* slammed onto an underwater shoal a short distance from the island. Perched precariously upon the rocks, wind struck the ship causing it to lurch sideways, and several of the straps securing the heavy coin-filled chests in the hull broke, shifting the chests to the port side. The sudden redistribution of weight caused the *Defense* to tip sideways even more. It began rapidly taking on water. Certain the ship was going down, the crew leapt into the violent sea and swam for the Fisher Island shore about two hundred yards away. Several drowned in the attempt.

By the time the survivors found shelter from the storm in the trees on the western shore, the *Defense* had broken free from its perch on the shoals and had begun drifting toward the southwest. As the *Defense* disappeared into the swirling storm, the captain observed that his ship continued taking on water and was riding dangerously low in the sea. During occasional lighting strikes that illuminated the open sea for a great distance, the *Defense* survivors, and eyewitnesses watching from Connecticut's south shore near what is known locally as Goshen Point, watched as the ship, its prow now submerged, continued floating southwestward and eventually out of sight. It was estimated the *Defense* went down in about fifty feet of water approximately five miles south of the coast and four miles southwest of Fisher Island.

War duties prevented a salvage attempt to recover the Continental dollars, and by the time the Revolution wound down, the sinking of the *Defense* was by and large forgotten by authorities and relegated to only a few pages in area journals and history books.

Attempts to retrieve the treasure during the late 1700s were foiled by the strong undercurrents that threatened the lives of divers. During the 1800s, fragments of the *Defense* were occasionally found on the beach at Goshen Point, reviving the tragic story of the ship's sinking and the lost treasure. Subsequent dives during the nineteenth century brought up more pieces of the ship and artifacts such as tools, pistols, and fittings, but no coins were ever located.

In 1956, Solomon Weaver accidentally encountered a reference to the tale that led him to undertake extensive research on the *Defense*, its cargo, and unfortunate sinking. Using the information derived from several weeks of study, Weaver actually found the remains of the wrecked ship. Several dives to the bottom were constantly plagued by the water's dangerous currents, and after three months, Weaver abandoned the project.

In 1977, a commercial salvor from New York made several attempts to explore the wreckage of the *Defense*, but he, like Weaver, remained at the mercy of the underwater turbulence and gave up the search.

Others have investigated the possibilities of retrieving the five hundred thousand silver coins only fifty feet below the surface.

Each time, however, they were discouraged by what they learned about the deadly swirling waters.

The precise value of the Continental dollars would be difficult to estimate, but it would no doubt be in the millions. One collector referred to them as "priceless." To the lucky salvor who can find a way to retrieve the coins, an incredible fortune awaits, a reward sufficient to make the dangerous effort worthwhile. Until some method is devised to conquer the threatening currents, however, the Continental dollars will very likely remain hidden in the sands of the Atlantic bottom.

NEW YORK

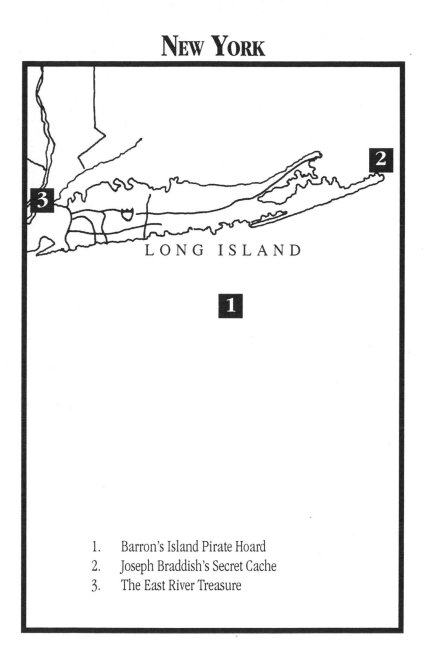

LONG ISLAND

Barron's Island Pirate Hoard

For ten years, pirate Charles Gibbs raided, looted, raped, and pillaged up and down the Atlantic seaboard and throughout the Caribbean Sea with a gang of ruthless and hardened cutthroats. Gibbs certainly lacked the flair and style of noted pirates such as Captain Kidd and Captain Braddish. Gibbs, in fact, was little more than a petty criminal who took to the sea. His methods were cowardly, and his successes generally depended on the work of others that he enlisted.

Gibbs definitely acquired treasure during his years of piracy. In fact, he amassed and spent a fortune, and was on his way to acquiring a second fortune when he was captured. In 1830, Gibbs successfully cached some of his treasure on New York's Barron's Island, but he was arrested and executed shortly afterward. To this day, his treasure remains hidden on the small island located not far from Long Island.

Charles Gibbs grew up as the son of a humble Rhode Island farmer. Deeply religious, the elder Gibbs made certain his wife and children attended church every Sunday and worked in the fields during the rest of the week. The young Gibbs cared little for the backbreaking labor of the farm or the strict and structured religious training, and at the first opportunity he ran away from home and enlisted in the navy.

Gibbs developed an early fascination with the sea and derived a certain pleasure from it that he never experienced from working on land. He soon found himself assigned to the *Chesapeake*, a navy warship commissioned to defend the coastal waters of the Middle Atlantic. During a battle with a British warship, Gibbs was taken prisoner and served a sentence in a Dartmoor prison. Historians believe that Gibbs grew attracted to a life of crime while in prison. Upon release, Gibbs tried his hand at petty thievery and various con games but was a failure. Eventually, he opened a tavern that catered to hoodlums and pirates. Intrigued by the colorful tales of raids and captured booty told to him by the seagoing brigands who frequented his place of business, Gibbs began longing to return to the sea.

In business only a few months, Gibbs's tavern was losing money at a steady rate, and the time seemed appropriate for him to pull up stakes and seek work on a ship. His first job was as a crewman on a South American privateer that escorted trading vessels through the dangerous, pirate-infested waters of the Caribbean and Atlantic. Following several losing encounters with well-armed pirate vessels, Gibbs began to believe that piracy offered more and better opportunities for adventure and riches than serving on a privateer.

For several weeks, Gibbs secretly met with selected members of the privateer's crew and plotted mutiny. When the time was appropriate, Gibbs convinced his followers to attack and kill the officers and dump their bodies overboard. Then, Gibbs appointed himself the captain of the ship, converted it into a pirate vessel, and in a short time was directing attacks on merchant vessels in the Caribbean Sea.

Much of Gibbs's reputation as a pirate resulted from his early depredations in the Caribbean. Purely out of mindless cruelty, Gibbs subjected his poor captives to horrible tortures that sometimes lasted for days before Gibbs finally ended the victims' misery. His reputation as a heartless, cowardly, and maniacal freebooter spread throughout the Caribbean, and soon fleets of American,

British, and French warships pursued him. Suffering constant harassment here, Gibbs decided to sail northward and turn his attention to pillaging ships and communities along the Atlantic Coast.

It didn't take long for Gibbs to become a wanted man in this new territory, and after being chased up and down the coast a number of times, he decided to retire from piracy before he was finally captured and hung.

After docking in Boston Harbor, Gibbs paid off his crew, sold his boat, and, loading his belongings and loot into several trunks, fled to England where he lived under an assumed name.

For two years, Gibbs enjoyed the life of the English leisure class but continued to long for adventure on the high seas. A heavy drinker and an obsessive gambler, Gibbs foolishly squandered his entire fortune and was forced to seek employment.

During the ensuing months, Gibbs worked on merchant vessels that visited ports in Europe, Africa, the Caribbean, as well as the Atlantic and Gulf coasts of America. In 1830, still using an alias, Gibbs signed on as a crewman of the *Vineyard*, a merchant vessel commanded by Captain William Thornby. Sailing out of the port of New Orleans, the *Vineyard* carried a heavy cargo of cotton, molasses, and several kegs containing fifty thousand in gold and silver coins minted in Mexico.

Reverting to his mutinous ways, Gibbs persuaded several crewmen and a steward, Thomas Wansley, to kill Captain Thornby and take control of the ship. On November 23 when the *Vineyard* was six days out of New Orleans, Wansley, along with four companions, attacked Thornby and crushed his skull with an iron rod. Watching from a hiding place, Gibbs rushed out when he was certain Thornby was dead and threw the corpse overboard. At that point, the first mate, accompanied by five sailors, tried to subdue Gibbs and Wansley. But the remaining crewmen who threw their allegiance to Gibbs came to the pirate's rescue and subdued the would-be defenders of the *Vineyard*. Gibbs took a macabre pleasure in chopping off the first mate's hands and throwing him into the ocean.

The next morning, following a night of drunken revelry, Gibbs ordered the *Vineyard* to proceed on to New York. Once in sight of land, Gibbs told his followers that he intended to remove the treasure from the vessel, bury it on Long Island, scuttle the ship, and return for the money about a month later.

When the *Vineyard* finally arrived off the coast of New York, Gibbs had it run aground on a sandbar, causing serious damage to the hull. After dividing the money with his crew and keeping twenty-five thousand for himself, Gibbs and his crew loaded themselves into longboats and rowed toward Long Island.

The longboats had been in the water only a few minutes when a squall overtook the men. The choppy waters and thickening fog disoriented the pirates, and time after time they became stuck on sandbars. Finally, after navigating through the dense fog by instinct, they arrived at a sandy beach. They unloaded the coin-filled kegs from the boats and buried them in separate holes dug in the sand several yards above the waterline.

Shortly after spotting the wrecked *Vineyard* on the sandbar, a lookout on an American gunboat that was patrolling the waters discovered several rowboats on a nearby shore. The gunboat's commander trekked ashore and found Gibbs and a dozen crewmen huddled against the growing storm under a makeshift shelter. Gibbs told the commander that the captain and first mate of the *Vineyard* fell into the sea and drowned when the ship ran aground. Fearful that the vessel was going to sink, Gibbs explained that he and the rest of the crew lowered the longboats and rowed to Long Island. On hearing this, the commander immediately informed Gibbs he had landed on Barron's Island, not Long Island.

Gibbs and his men were given directions to the home of a Barron's Island resident named Johnson who, the commander said, would give them fresh water and food and help get them to the mainland. While encamped on the island for the next few days, Jack Brownrigg, one of Gibbs's mutineers, confided to Johnson how the *Vineyard*'s captain and first mate were killed and how Gibbs had run the ship onto the sandbar. He also informed Johnson about the buried treasure on the beach. At the first opportunity, Johnson alerted the local constable who arrested all the pirates.

After Gibbs and his accomplices were apprehended, Johnson and the constable went to the beach where Brownrigg claimed the treasure was buried. Tidal surges had obliterated any evidence of recent excavation, and, though they probed into the sands throughout the area, nothing was found.

Following a lengthy trial, Gibbs and Wansley were hanged, and the rest were sent to prison for life. Since Charles Gibbs's execution, controversy has existed with regard to whether or not it was actually Barron's Island where the pirates landed. In 1860, an anonymous researcher and writer claimed the loot was hidden on nearby Pelican Island, and still others maintain Great Barron Island is where the coins were cached.

All of the available evidence, however, points to Barron's Island as the actual location of the treasure. Furthermore, in 1986, a gold coin was found on the beach along the southern shore of Barron's Island. After it had been cleaned and examined by a collector, it was positively identified as being of Mexican origin.

The $50,000 in gold coins hidden on the Barron's Island beach in 1830 by Gibbs and his pirates is worth considerably more today, and it is highly probable that persistent searching with sophisticated electronic detection equipment could yield positive results.

Joseph Braddish's Secret Cache

Only days before his capture in Rhode Island in 1699, Joseph Braddish concealed approximately one-third of a million dollars' worth of coins and jewels on Montauk Point, the easternmost tip of Long Island.

Braddish's fate with his Block Island cache in Rhode Island forever plunged the location of his Montauk Point treasure into deep mystery, for neither Braddish nor his crew were able to return for it and subsequent severe storms have altered landmarks. The treasure, consisting of booty taken from several raids on merchant vessels, is still hidden somewhere on the island.

On his way to the noted Block Island pirate hideout just south of the Rhode Island shore, Braddish's first mate on the *Adventure* notified him of a growing problem with the tiller. At that point, the *Adventure* was sailing past Long Island's Montauk Point, only twenty-five miles from their destination. Not wishing to risk the navigation of Block Island Sound with a faulty rudder, Braddish ordered the ship anchored just off the eastern tip of Long Island at a place called Montauk Point. While crewmen worked on the tiller, Braddish and several others rowed to shore.

Walking about the beach, Braddish encountered several sites he deemed suitable for hiding some of his treasure. Always a practical pirate, Braddish did not like the idea of caching his entire wealth in one single location, preferring instead to distribute it among several. Montauk Point appeared ideal as a hiding place.

Braddish confessed his intentions to the three sailors who accompanied him in the longboat, and invited their participation in a scheme to remove some of the treasure aboard the *Adventure* and cache it on the island.

Around midnight, Braddish and the sailors crept into the hold of the *Adventure*, opened one of the trunks containing booty, and removed approximately three hundred thousand dollars' worth of gold and silver coins along with some gems and jewelry. Wrapping and tying the treasure in pieces of canvas sailcloth, the four men carried the bundles topside and loaded them into a longboat. Several trips from the hull to the deck were required to transport the loot.

After untying and pushing off from the *Adventure*, the pirates, directed by Braddish, rowed to the location on Montauk Point where they had beached the previous day, believed to be on the northeastern shore.

Once ashore, Braddish led the men to a site he considered ideal for hiding the treasure—a location midway between the shore and a small inland pond. Here, the men excavated a large, deep hole and deposited the bundles of treasure. After filling in the hole and obliterating any sign of excavation, Braddish paced off the distance from the cache to the shoreline, made note of the direction, and returned to the longboat. Within thirty minutes, Braddish and the sailors were back aboard the *Adventure*.

On the afternoon of the following day, the tiller was finally repaired and the *Adventure* sailed on to Block Island.

Braddish, captured by the authorities days later and eventually executed in England for his piratical activities, never returned to Montauk Point. The existence of the hidden buried treasure would never be known if one of the sailors who accompanied Braddish had not told the story to his Newport jailer. The jailer, thinking he would travel to Long Island and retrieve the treasure for himself, kept the information secret for several weeks. His conscience got the better of him, however, and he eventually related the story to his superior. No measures were ever taken to search for the Montauk Point treasure and it was soon forgotten.

Years later, the jailer's diary was found in a storeroom containing several hand-written pages detailing the caching of Joseph Braddish's treasure at Montauk Point on Long Island. The diary was eventually turned over to a local storekeeper who became intrigued at the possibility of finding Braddish's buried cache of coins and jewels.

Outfitting himself with a small but sturdy sailboat, the storekeeper, with the help of two companions, sailed from Newport to Montauk Point. On arriving at the northeastern shore, he constantly consulted the diary and checked the surroundings for landmarks. After exploring around the area for nearly two hours, the three men came upon the pond about one-half mile from the shore. After returning to the shoreline, the storekeeper paced off two hundred and seventy-seven steps back in the direction of the pond and placed a marker. He pointed at the marker and told his companions that was where the treasure was buried.

Though they dug a hole nearly six feet deep and eight feet wide, they found nothing. Over and over, the storekeeper referred to the diary and paced off the distance, each time arriving at the same location, but there was no treasure. The next day, the three men returned to Rhode Island.

After word of his failure spread throughout the town, the storekeeper was paid a visit one day by a very old man. From his appearance, the old-timer was a veteran of several decades at sea, and he claimed he possessed information about Montauk Point that gave the storekeeper renewed hope. Several years earlier, he explained, a severe storm struck the eastern end of Long Island and inflicted great damage. High waves surged across Montauk

Point, eroding beaches and carrying away tons of sand. The configuration of Montauk Point's northeastern shoreline was completely rearranged, according to the old man, with several dozen feet of it having been removed completely.

The storekeeper's morale was boosted by this piece of information, and he made arrangements for a return expedition to Montauk Point. After arriving the second time, he decided he was no better off than before, because he had no idea of the location of the shoreline at the time the treasure was buried. The few residents in the area he asked could not remember. Once again, the storekeeper returned to Newport and never ventured to Montauk Point again.

The East River Treasure

On November 23, 1780, the H.M.S. *Hussar* struck a submerged rock outcrop in the East River and sank seventy-five feet into the water. Its cargo partially consisted of one to two million in gold and silver coins intended as payroll funds for British troops stationed in New York.

The *Hussar*, a one hundred fourteen feet long British Navy frigate, was constructed seventeen years earlier. When it arrived in the New York harbor, it carried twenty-eight guns, a crew of two hundred, a compliment of soldiers, and several American prisoners' who had been shipped from prison camps in England and were to be exchanged for captured British soldiers. Historians argue that the soldiers were on board to guard the payroll and not the prisoners.

The *Hussar*'s captain was nervous about anchoring in the New York harbor. Many believed the French were intent on capturing the ship. A fleet of French warships was known to be as close as Rhode Island. Furthermore, at least six thousand French soldiers transporting artillery, along with several companies of American troops, were converging on New York City. An attack was imminent.

Because of the danger to the *Hussar* and its valuable cargo, the captain, along with General Clinton, the British commander of New York, decided the ship should sail to a safer location as soon as possible. Eventually, everyone agreed to proceed to Connecticut.

The fastest route to Connecticut was up the East River and across the calm waters of Long Island Sound, and several British warships anchored along the way could provide protection if needed. The alternative was to sail parallel to the south shore of Long Island, but the prevailing southerly winds forced ships to sail into positions far out to sea to avoid being blown onto the beach. Such an extended route was time-consuming and would also expose the *Hussar* to potential attack from roving French warships.

Sailing from New York harbor up the East River and into Long Island Sound, though a militarily sound decision, was also fraught with problems. Tricky currents, along with several submerged rock outcrops, had sunk many ships in this river.

The captain of the *Hussar* appointed a local man to navigate the ship up the river. The new pilot, though experienced with the route, advised against taking the ship through the East River waters. The captain, convinced he had little choice in the matter, ordered the pilot to proceed anyway.

After leaving the New York harbor, the *Hussar* passed by the southern tip of Manhattan Island and up the East River. Passing to the east of Welfare Island, a narrow, two-mile long strip of land in the middle of the river, the swift current created problems for the ship, and it took the effort of several crewmen to hold it to its course in the middle of the channel.

Just beyond Welfare Island, the East River flowed through the aptly named Hell Gate where the tidal waters of Long Island Sound mixed with those of the stream. Those swirling currents have caused many ships to be slammed against rocky islands and shoreline bluffs. Treacherous granite ledges also extended into the river, some just inches below the water's surface.

Soon after entering Hell Gate, the *Hussar* slammed into one of the ledges. Pot Rock, as it is known locally, lay only eighteen inches below the surface, but the eddying stream, thick with silt, hid the rock from the view of the lookout. With stunning impact, the *Hussar* smacked broadside into Pot Rock, splitting several hull timbers.

Taking the wheel from the pilot, the captain steered the ship off the rocks and back out into the river. From the pilothouse, he could see the Stony Point Beach on Bronx's south shore. Returning the wheel to the pilot, the captain ordered him to head directly for the beach and shallow water. The pilot took the wheel, and the captain went below deck to survey the damage.

It was worse than he feared. Water was gushing at a frightening rate through several tears in the hull, and the ship was already listing to one side. Fearful that the payroll might never be recovered if sunk in these treacherous waters, the captain prayed for a safe landing at Stony Point Beach as he returned to the pilothouse.

Only moments later, the *Hussar*, now almost completely filled with water, stopped moving forward and rocked helplessly in the river. Crewmen lowered rowboats into the stream and quickly crowded into them. As the last of the boats rowed away from the *Hussar*, the frigate went straight down. When the sailors finally reached the nearby shore, they turned back toward the river and saw only the tops of the *Hussar*'s masts extending above the water.

Several crewmen volunteered to retrieve the payroll, but the treacherous waters proved too dangerous. During the next several years, the British were at war, and no organized attempts were made to recover the treasure.

In 1819, the first serious attempt to reach the payroll occurred. Few details are available, but it is known that several cannons and cannonballs were raised, along with numerous metal fittings and other ship accouterments. A number of coins were also found, but the bulk of the treasure eluded the searchers.

During the 1820s, another salvage team arrived trying to locate and retrieve the payroll. After rowing out into the river above the wreck, workers dropped a large grappling hook with cable attached to the hull. From the nearby shore, the hook was winched back. Several more artifacts were recovered, but the wooden chests carrying the coins were never snagged.

In 1832, a British salvage company appeared in New York and announced it would attempt to recover the lost payroll from the bottom of the East River. The team's leader said they intended to employ a newly invented diving bell, but the swift and unpredictable currents disrupted control of the device. After several unsuccessful attempts, the British packed up and went home.

As time passed, more and more ships fell prey to the treacherous rocks of Hell Gate. Eventually, the river bottom was littered with the hulls of wrecked ships, and it became difficult to determine which was the *Hussar*.

The Worcester Hussar Company, another British salvage team, set up camp on the eastern shore of the river opposite the presumed wreck site in 1856. They carried documented information gleaned from British archives that stated the *Hussar* had been transporting $1.8 million in gold and silver coins when it sank. Other documents discovered a decade later set the amount at two million and still other materials uncovered after the turn of the century referred to only one million. The Worcester Hussar Company encountered the same difficulties as previous salvage teams and gave up after only a few days.

In 1937, Simon Lake, an inventor, constructed a tiny submarine to search the bottom of the East River, but he had no luck in locating the *Hussar*.

If the formidable obstacle of the dangerous river currents could be overcome, a fortune in gold and silver coins awaits a sophisticated recovery attempt at the bottom of the East River not far from the shore of Astoria Park. Estimated to be worth considerably more than $20 million today, the value of this treasure could definitely make the effort worthwhile.

NEW JERSEY

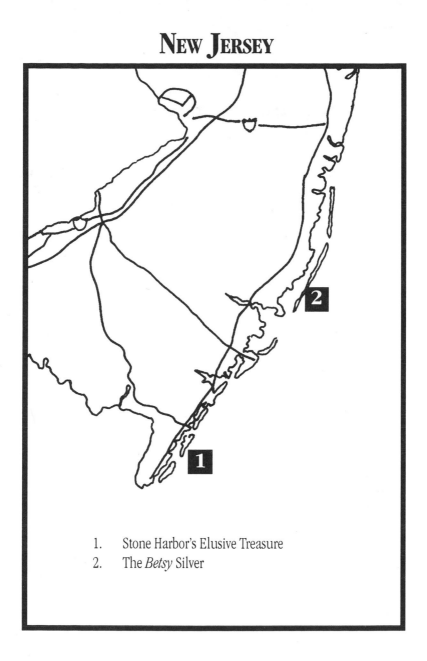

Stone Harbor's Elusive Treasure

On the Atlantic Ocean side of New Jersey's southern tip lies the small town of Stone Harbor, a quiet community with twelve hundred residents. Geographically, Stone Harbor sits on a barrier island, separated from the mainland by a shallow lagoon known as Jenkins Sound. In 1710, a treasure chest was buried somewhere along the Stone Harbor beach, and to this day the location and chest's contents, as well as the men who buried it, remain a mystery.

During the early 1700s, few residents lived on the long, narrow, sandy barrier island now known as Seven Mile Beach. One of them, a retired seaman named Captain Eli Barnett, who went to sea as a thirteen year old, was in his sixties and manned a rescue station near the southwestern end of Seven Mile Beach. He always kept a close and constant watch on the nearby Atlantic Ocean for ships.

For hours each day, Barnett scanned the ocean and the beach through an old telescope that he had salvaged from the last ship he served. Around dawn one morning during late spring of 1710, Barnett spotted a dark three-masted vessel approaching the island from the east. After anchoring approximately one-half mile off-shore, a rowboat was dropped into the water, and a large and very heavy wooden chest was lowered into it by ropes and pulleys. As Barnett observed this activity through his telescope, he noticed the ship flying a flag with a skull and crossbones. Finally, five men entered the boat and rowed toward the shore.

Watching the pirates from his low frame hut in a tiny grove of trees, Barnett began to grow concerned when the rowboat landed on the sandy shore. One of the men, apparently the one in command, climbed out of the boat and walked up and down the beach making note of landmarks. The pirate did not notice Barnett's humble habitation approximately a quarter of a mile away, and he simply turned back toward the rowboat and ordered the others to remove the chest.

Pointing the way, the leader directed his fellows to follow him with the chest. As the four pirates labored with the great load, they tried to keep up with their companion, and eventually the entire party disappeared from Barnett's view behind a large sand dune. One of the pirates soon returned to the rowboat, removed two shovels, and hustled back to the far side of the dune. An hour later, the five men reappeared without the chest and, after climbing into the rowboat, returned to the ship.

Barnett, fighting a burning curiosity to see what was in the chest, wanted to go search for it. Instead, he remained in his hut, fearful he might be spotted walking along the beach by the ship's lookout.

Early the next morning gathering clouds in the northeast promised a storm. The rowboat, however, reappeared on the beach. As Barnett watched, the same five men, two of whom were carrying shovels, left the boat and hiked once again around the dune, presumably to the same spot where they hid the chest the previous day.

Another hour passed before the pirates returned. After conversing briefly, they entered the rowboat and returned to the ship. Later that afternoon, as the sky grew darker and the winds increased in intensity, the ship hoisted anchor and sailed away over the horizon.

Barnett was determined to follow the pirate's tracks to the spot where the chest was hidden, but as he donned his coat and pulled on his boots, the storm struck the island. Heavy rain and strong winds pummelled Barnett's little shack until he thought it would blow apart. Huddled in one corner of the structure, the old seaman waited out the tempest.

For three days the rain fell. Finally the clouds parted enough to allow the sun to brighten the barrier island landscape. With a stiff wind still blowing, Barnett pulled down his hat, turned up his collar, and walked out onto the beach.

The storm had obliterated the pirate's tracks, but Barnett easily retraced their route to the point where they had vanished behind the dune. From here, however, no clue revealed their destination. For the next two hours, Barnett searched the area for some evidence of an excavation but could find none.

For weeks, the old seaman revisited the region behind the dune, trying to find some evidence of where the chest could have been buried. Occasionally, he dug into what he considered a likely spot but came away empty-handed.

Barnett lived on the Seven Mile Beach island for another ten years. Though he continued to search for what he believed to be a pirate treasure, its location eluded him. In time, he told the story to others who came to search, but the cache was never found.

What could possibly have been in the heavy chest? During the 1700s, it is unlikely that pirates would have taken the trouble to bury anything unless it was valuable, and judging from Barnett's observation of the chest's extremely heavy weight, it would be fair to guess that it contained either gold, silver, or jewels, or a combination of each. And what was the reason for the return of the pirates the following day? Did they move the chest to a different location? Or did they add booty to the treasure cache?

Until discovered, the contents remain a puzzle, but an event that occurred in 1944 sheds some light on the treasure.

One summer Sunday of that year, the Youngs of Atlantic City, along with their three children, were visiting relatives in the nearby town of Swainton. Around midmorning, they decided to pack a lunch, take the short drive to Stone Harbor, and picnic on the beach. Seated on blankets and eating sandwiches, the parents watched their children play and romp in the surf. Presently tiring of the water, the youngsters retired to the beach behind a nearby dune to dig in the sand and build sand castles.

After three hours, the family returned to Swainton, and that evening the Youngs went home to Atlantic City. The next day after Mr. Young left for work, Mrs. Young gathered her children's dirty clothes to wash. As she was going through the pockets of her youngest son's trousers, she pulled out five strange coins. When she asked the youth where they came from, he told her he took them out of a box he had found in the sand while playing the previous day. The box, he said, was filled with the coins.

That evening when Mr. Young came home, his wife showed him the coins. Intrigued, Young took them to a noted Atlantic City coin collector for examination. After a thick residue was cleaned from the objects, the collector discovered that they were Spanish in origin and minted from nearly pure gold in 1706!

The following week, Young returned to Seven Mile Beach with his son to try and relocate the box filled with gold coins. Though they spent hours combing the area, nothing was found. Their search spurred local interest in the likelihood that pirate treasure might be buried nearby, and throughout the next several weeks, hundreds of treasure hunters arrived in the area to try and find the cache. In all, two dozen gold coins were found, all similar to those in Young's possession, and it was presumed they were dropped earlier by the children, who were playing with them. The chest, however, was never found.

Though unproven, it seems likely that the gold coins were part of that huge elusive treasure cached by pirates nearly three hundred years earlier.

The *Betsy* Silver

In 1778, the British ship *Betsy* completed an Atlantic crossing and was in sight of New Jersey's Long Island when a nor'easter struck. The fierce winds and high waves associated with these severe storms terrorized even the most veteran seamen, and hundreds of ships litter the bottom of the upper Atlantic Coast as result of such gales. The *Betsy*, carrying a large cargo of goods along with an estimated $1.5 million in silver coins, fell victim to this storm, and sank beneath the surging sea, carrying its treasure to the continental shelf's floor.

When the captain of the *Betsy* spied the oncoming storm, he decided to navigate the ship into shallower and safer waters. He gave orders to lower the sails, drop anchor, and wait out the storm. Barely recognizing the low, linear shape of Long Island on the western horizon, he steered toward it, hoping for refuge in the sound between it and the mainland.

As the skies darkened and the winds increased, the *Betsy* held a course straight for the old Beach Haven Inlet. Once through the inlet and into Little Egg Harbor just beyond, the ship would be protected, but only minutes away from the shallow inlet, the *Betsy* unsuccessfully fought the strong winds and was forced upon a shoal that shattered several hull timbers. Foundering just offshore, the ship took on water at a great rate and went down, carrying cargo and silver along with it. Only six of the crew managed to swim to safety.

It was months before the sunken shipment of silver coins became public knowledge, but when it did, several enterprising fortune seekers attempted to locate the wreck and retrieve the treasure. The task proved to be more difficult than anticipated.

No one ever positively identified the wreck, but more detrimental to a successful recovery operation was the tidal movement in this part of the Atlantic. Strong tides have always surged into and out of this area rapidly, generating dangerous, swirling currents. The churning waters carry such a heavy load of sand that visibility for the most part is extremely limited. Due to the strong tidal surges, experts maintain that less than one hour a day would be available for an actual recovery.

Since the *Betsy* went down in 1778, at least fifty formal attempts have been made to locate it, all unsuccessful. But evidence of the offshore wreck's existence and its treasure, however, is abundant. Since the *Betsy* sank, the hull, decks, and masts have experienced considerable rotting. It is also probable that the wooden chests carrying the fortune in silver coins have also succumbed to the weathering process, freeing the contents to spill into the ocean's sands.

Since the 1940s, beachcombers have picked up silver coins along Beach Haven Beach that could only have come from the *Betsy* shipment. During the past fifty years, hundreds of coins have been recovered, leading researchers to believe that the wreck of the *Betsy* is located only a short distance offshore. The temptation to locate the old ship and try to recover the remainder of the coins is great, but the dangerous waters still keep salvors away.

All but one. It is possible that a longtime Long Island resident has finally discovered the remains of the *Betsy*. The man, who desires anonymity, is a diver with a long record of success in retrieving artifacts from sunken wrecks. Though he claims to have identified the *Betsy* from ballast stones and mast stumps near the old inlet, he refuses to respond to direct questions about the silver coins.

Assuming the bulk of the huge shipment of silver coins still lies amidst the *Betsy*'s remains, it would be far more than a single diver could likely recover, given the hazardous underwater environment. The notion that this wealth is there for the taking appeals to many possessing a spirit of adventure. The treasure of the *Betsy*, worth several million dollars today, continues to lure and confound.

Delaware

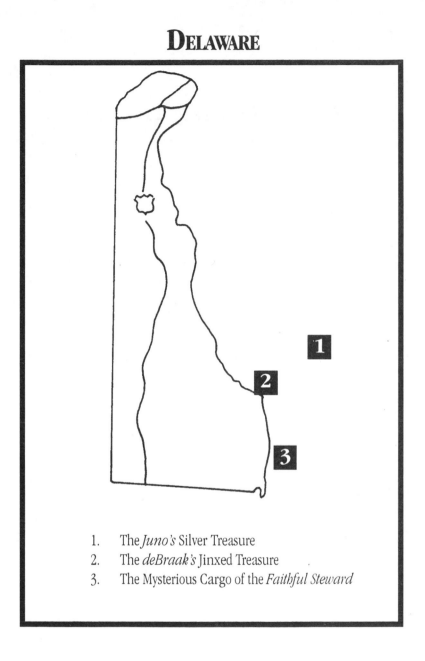

1. The *Juno's* Silver Treasure
2. The *deBraak's* Jinxed Treasure
3. The Mysterious Cargo of the *Faithful Steward*

The *Juno's* Silver Treasure

Having just experienced a difficult and stormy Atlantic Ocean voyage from Veracruz, Mexico, to offshore Delaware, the Spanish ship *Juno* fought a fierce gale as seawater surged into growing leaks in the hull. Already riding low in the water as a result of transporting a cargo of silver bullion weighing twelve tons, the *Juno* finally broke apart and sank to the bottom, carrying its treasure along with four hundred and thirty-one sailors, crewmen, officers, and troops. For days, an American ship searched the sea for survivors but found none.

In January 1802, the Spanish frigate *Juno*, loaded with hundreds of silver ingots, departed the port of Veracruz bound for Spain. In the ship's hold, an incredible treasure consisting of twelve tons of silver bullion was stacked. Close to bankruptcy, Spain desperately needed the silver in its fight to maintain control over several independence-minded colonies. The silver was to be carried to the country where it would be added to the coffers of the motherland's treasury.

Sailing side-by-side in the Caribbean Sea with another Spanish frigate, the *Anfitrite*, the *Juno* suffered several serious leaks and revised its route in order to dock in San Juan, Puerto Rico, for repairs to the hull. The *Juno*, one hundred and seventy feet long and sporting a number of cannons, carried a huge amount of passengers, most of them Spanish troops who were returning to Europe. Captain Don Ignacio Bustillo, a veteran of numerous Atlantic crossings, commanded the ship.

Once in port at San Juan, Bustillo's examination of the *Juno*'s hull led him to declare the vessel unseaworthy, and several months passed before the ship was able to sail.

The delay placed the *Juno* and the *Anfitrite* in the paths of unfavorable winds that made sailing eastward difficult at those latitudes. Bustillo elected to sail northward toward Bermuda and take advantage of more favorable winds. Though the revised route was hundreds of miles out of the way, it was ultimately safer because the captain was growing concerned over the great load of silver and the men aboard the *Juno*. If a severe ocean storm occurred, the overloaded ship would not fare well.

Near Bermuda, several days of fog followed by heavy rains separated the two vessels, and the *Juno* continued sailing north-westward toward the North American coast in search of better winds.

On October 22, a strong gale snapped one of the *Juno*'s masts and blew the mainsail out to sea. On the same day, several major new leaks opened up in the hull, and by nightfall the hold was six feet deep in seawater.

The next day, the captain assigned all of the crew and most of the soldiers to bail water from the hull as they filled cracks in the timbers and seams with caulking and tar. The efforts reduced the leakage somewhat, but on the following morning several new breaks appeared.

Already riding dangerously low in the water, Captain Bustillos ordered the bow anchors and all of the cannons thrown overboard to lighten the load. Eventually, sails were removed from the remaining masts and draped around the outside portions of the hull in an attempt to inhibit leakage.

As the *Juno*'s crew struggled to make repairs and remain afloat in the growing storm, an American schooner, the *Favorite*, approached and offered assistance.

On October 25, a contingent from the *Juno* rowed to the *Favorite* and requested an escort to an American port so that repairs could be made to the Spanish ship. By October 27, the two vessels were approximately two hundred miles southeast of Cape May, New Jersey, and sailing toward the safety of Delaware Bay.

That evening, another violent storm blew up, threatening to destroy the *Juno* once and for all. As the crew of the Spanish ship fought to plug new leaks in ten feet of rising water, the *Favorite* suffered the loss of a sail and was experiencing difficulty maintaining its position.

For two more days, the American sailors fought the storm along with the Spaniards. As the sailors on the *Favorite* watched, another of the *Juno*'s masts snapped and its rudder broke off and floated away, leaving the ship entirely at the mercy of the raging sea. In the distance, the Americans could hear the Spaniards, crowded onto the deck of the *Juno*, shouting for help.

The *Favorite*'s captain tried to navigate his unwieldy vessel toward the *Juno* and attempt a rescue. However, the loss of the sail along with the strong winds prevented it from occurring. Dense rains poured onto the ships from the low, dark clouds, and sometime during the night the *Juno* and the *Favorite* became separated. It was the last time the *Juno* was ever seen. The American captain estimated the two ships were approximately twenty-five miles due east of the mouth of Delaware Bay at the time.

The following morning the storm had finally passed and the skies had cleared. The *Favorite* sailed about the area in search of the Spanish frigate, but it was nowhere to be found. The captain eventually filed a report that the *Juno* went down in ninety feet of water on the night of October 27.

The twelve tons of silver carried by the *Juno*, all in the form of ingots, was valued at approximately $400,000 in 1802 values.

Today, the silver would be worth considerably more, and the historical and artifact value is immeasurable.

It was not until sometime in the 1880s that researchers learned about the *Juno*'s cargo. Employing the 1802 captain's log of the *Favorite*, which was discovered in a Boston library, the potential site of the wreck was identified, and several salvage attempts were made to find the silver. Recovery methods were crude; the efforts failed.

During the 1960s, a diver and part-time salvage operator from New Jersey claimed to have located the remains of the *Juno*, and as proof he showed several silver ingots with Spanish markings that he claimed he brought up from the continental shelf.

According to the salvor, the treasure was considerably less than twenty-five miles east of the mouth of Delaware Bay, and it lay in only forty feet of water. The New Jersey man intended to retrieve the rest of the ingots, he said, when he had funding for a full-time recovery operation. As he lined up investors for the project, however, the salvor, a sixty-three year old man with a history of health problems, suffered a severe heart attack and died before revealing the exact location of the *Juno*'s silver.

The location still remains a puzzle to this day.

The *deBraak*'s Jinxed Treasure

While waiting out a storm a few hundred yards off Delaware's Cape Henlopen, the British sloop *deBraak* sat dangerously low in the water because of its heavy cargo. Stacked both above and below decks was an immense treasure in gold and silver coins and ingots, most of it accumulated during recent raids in the Caribbean.

As the *deBraak*'s Captain James Drew ordered his crewmen to redistribute the load of treasure chests and stacks of ingots, a sudden gale blew up, caught the still-raised sails, and caused the ship, already overloaded and starboard-heavy, to heel over and sink. Captain Drew, along with thirty-seven crewmen, perished, and a treasure estimated to be worth between $25 million and $50 million went to the bottom. Because of what many claim to be a jinx, the treasure has eluded searchers for nearly two hundred years.

Even the cutter *deBraak*, as well as its cargo of treasure, was believed to have been jinxed, and mysterious events and circumstances associated with both have served to reinforce such notions.

The *deBraak* was originally constructed in Holland in 1787, and before it was launched a bizarre series of accidents killed eight of the Javanese workers over a six-week period. Even then, workers complained about a jinx attached to the ship, and they feared to approach it. During its first week at sea, the *deBraak* sprung leaks in several places and had to return to port for repairs. During its second voyage, it was captured by the French in Buzzards Bay near Falmouth, Massachusetts. The French immediately placed it into service as a warship, and, while on its first mission under a new flag, the *deBraak* was seized by the British in 1798.

The *deBraak*'s reputation as a jinxed ship was growing, and by this time it was well-known in the Atlantic and up and down the east coast. Under escort from the *H.M.S. Fortune*, the vessel was towed into Plymouth Harbor where it was closely inspected. After deeming the ship to be completely seaworthy, the British commissioned it into the Royal Navy as a sloop of war and assigned James Drew as its captain.

The *deBraak* was unique among ships of the day, for it was constructed of Javanese teak, a material found in no other ship in the Atlantic at the time. Although relatively small—one hundred twenty-five feet by thirty feet—for a warship, it was highly maneuverable. The ship's armament consisted of sixteen short bronze cannonades with large caliber. These short cannons, all bolted to the upper deck, were intended for short range assault and fired iron projectiles. Captain Drew was impressed with the *deBraak* and anxious to put it to a test.

Drew's desires were soon realized. On February 8, 1798, he received orders to sail the *deBraak* to the West Indies where it was to harass Spanish ships and seize their cargoes.

On arriving in the West Indies, the *deBraak* immediately encountered the *Commerce of London*, a Spanish vessel bound for Spain and transporting a large shipment of gold and silver. Following a brief battle, the *Commerce of London* was captured, and its treasure loaded into the hold of the victorious *deBraak*.

Several days later, the *deBraak* sailed into port at Jamaica to get supplies of food and water. While there, several British businessmen begged Captain Drew to take on a large amount of gold and ship it to England on its next transatlantic voyage. Drew agreed, and another large cargo was placed in the hold atop the Spanish treasure. While in port, Drew also received orders to sail for Halifax, Nova Scotia.

After leaving Jamaica for the North Atlantic, the *deBraak* encountered four more Spanish ships. Each was captured, and their shipments of gold and silver coins and ingots were transferred into the British ship. Drew grew concerned that the *deBraak* was overloaded, but he considered how his great victories and seizures would be received by his commanding officers, and was determined to deliver the booty to British headquarters.

On the first day of May 1798, the Spanish ship *San Francisco Xavier* was spotted by one of the *deBraak*'s lookouts, and Drew gave the order to pursue it. The Spanish vessel offered no resistance and flew the flag of surrender as the British approached. While inspecting the *San Francisco Xavier*'s cargo, Drew was surprised and delighted to discover a tremendous freight of gold and silver ingots along with several wooden chests filled with jewels. Having no more room in the *deBraak*'s hold, Drew's crewmen were forced to stack the treasure on the deck. Dangerously overloaded and lying very low in the water, the ship continued on to Nova Scotia, and all the while Drew prayed they would encounter no storms.

On May 25, the *deBraak* arrived just off the point of Delaware's Cape Henlopen, then called Cape James. Intending to rest here for two days while replenishing the water supply, Drew dropped anchor and was in the process of having the mainsail lowered when a sudden storm blew up. Within minutes, the violent storm rocked the *deBraak* to and fro, and the ship began filling with water. Drew, concerned about the great weight of the treasure stacked on the ship's starboard side, barked orders to have some of it redistributed when a sudden violent gust of wind capsized the vessel. Within seconds, the *deBraak*, carrying thirty-seven men and a massive fortune in treasure, sank to the bottom of the bay.

While the *deBraak* had fared well during several successful encounters with enemy ships, many believed that the jinx that had plagued the vessel during its early years rose to afflict it once more, causing the sinking. Though the warship now lay on the sands at the bottom of the bay, the jinx apparently remained with it, because each of the more than one dozen formal attempts to salvage the treasure in relatively calm, shallow waters encountered difficulties.

Three days after the *deBraak* sank, British military officials discussed the possibility of raising it. The distractions of war, however, caused the project to be abandoned. Six months later in November 1798, the *H.M.S. Hind* was assigned to find the *deBraak* and attempt retrieval of the treasure. After divers located the wreck, several attempts were made to pinpoint the ingots and chests, but after four days of searching they only recovered the bow anchor. The *Hind* spent another forty-eight days in the area, but a number of violent storms hampered salvage efforts. Finally, *Hind* Captain Larcomb withdrew, claiming the wreck a jinx.

In 1814, the British decided to attempt retrieving the treasure once again. The ship *Resolute* sailed to Delaware Bay to take up where the *Hind* left off, but as before, severe storms plagued the operation and caused it to be called off after one week.

In 1877, a consortium of New York and Philadelphia businessmen financed a salvage operation called the Pancoast Expedition. Their aim was to bring up the *deBraak*'s treasure from the bay's bottom, but from the first day, mechanical problems and bad weather inhibited recovery efforts.

Between 1880 and 1882, a group called the International Submarine Company attempted to raise the wreckage, but as with the 1877 attempt, they were beset with equipment breakdown and violent storms. After several weeks with nothing to show for their efforts, the ISC left the area.

In 1888, Jeff Townsend, a retired seaman from New Jersey, arrived at the coastal town of Lewes with a team of twelve professional divers. During their first effort, a chain identified as belonging to the *deBraak* was found. After following the chain along the bottom for about one hundred feet, it disappeared under the sand, and no amount of towing could pull it free. After spending another full week investigating the area around the chain, Townsend concluded that the *deBraak* was buried under at least twenty feet of sand and was impossible to recover.

While a United States Navy minesweeper was patrolling the waters of Delaware Bay in 1917, crewmen discovered a cannonade in the bottom sands. The small cannon was similar to the kind installed on the *deBraak*. The discovery was reported, but the document was buried under stacks of war-related missives, and eventually it was lost altogether.

In 1932, the Baltimore Derrick and Salvage Corporation decided to locate and retrieve the *deBraak*'s treasure. Led by professional diver and salvor Charles Jackson, two salvage boats and a one hundred ton derrick vessel were anchored off Cape Henlopen. Arriving at Delaware Bay, the BD & SC members heard talk from Lewes residents of the jinx that plagued the *deBraak* and every effort to locate the treasure. The salvage crew members, all hardened seamen with many years combined experience and not given to superstitions, merely laughed at what they considered a silly belief.

After three days of searching, several pieces of wood identified as being from the *deBraak* were brought up, and after pinpointing the underwater site, the salvage ships passed back and forth across it with draglines hoping to snare the wreck. Presently, one of the ships reported its line was caught on something, and Jackson, after donning his diving gear, was lowered to investigate.

By the time Jackson reached the floor of the bay, a violent storm struck the waters above, and the salvage ships had difficulty maintaining their positions. One of the boats was nearly capsized, and in the other ship's engine room—the one where Jackson was tethered—a drum of oil exploded, causing a blazing fire. While the boat burned furiously, several crew members hauled Jackson up from below, and moments later everyone was forced to evacuate to the second ship. Within an hour, the vessel burned to the waterline. Talk of the jinx now became common among the salvage crew, and no one laughed.

Two months later, the Baltimore Derrick and Salvage Corporation was still hard at work. Jackson and another diver, George Tyzack, found a wreck half-buried in the bottom sands that they believed was the *deBraak*. After examining the hulk, a few lengths of timbers were cut from it and several metal fittings were retrieved. Experts who subsequently examined the materials determined the wood was teak and the fittings dated to a time consistent with the building of the *deBraak*.

Encouraged by these findings, Jackson and Tyzack returned to Cape Henlopen, but the subsequent three weeks of searching were hampered by violent storms. Eventually, the Baltimore Derrick and Salvage Corporation opted to abandon the search.

On learning of the elusive treasure of the *deBraak* lying in Delaware Bay off Cape Henlopen, famed New York engineer Alfred Jordan undertook extensive research into the ship's history and its sinking. Claiming to have found a sea chart that noted the wreck's exact location, Jordan assembled a group of financiers, all successful businessmen with extensive shipping investments. After purchasing and outfitting a state-of-the-art recovery ship and hiring several experienced salvers, the group with supreme confidence commenced its search for the *deBraak* in March 1933.

Difficulty arose when the salvage team discovered not one sunken ship, but more than two dozen. After months of examining several of the wrecks and finding nothing of value, Jordan called off the search.

In 1935, a group from Rhode Island called the Colstad Expedition came to Lewes and made preparations to search for the *deBraak*. Like other searchers before them, they heard stories of the jinx but placed no store in such talk. Expedition members told Lewes residents that the reason other salvage efforts failed was because they undertook their searches during the storm season. After studying meteorological charts of the area, Colstad Expedition members determined to conduct their salvage activities when there was no chance of severe weather. Two days later, the salvage boat were anchored off Cape Henlopen, and the team made preparations to search the bottom. Early the following morning, however, an unexpected storm struck the area, and the resulting high winds and waves forced temporary abandonment of the project. Throughout the rest of the year, the Colstad Expedition returned to Delaware Bay several times to renew its attempt at searching for the *deBraak*, and each time it was repelled by stormy weather. The jinx, according to Lewes residents, had struck again!

Though discouraged, members of the Colstad Expedition returned to the bay during the summer of 1936. This time, they brought an eighteen-ton trawler that they used to sweep the bay back and forth hoping to locate the *deBraak*. About one week after commencing this new salvage operation, the trawler brought up a piece of teakwood. Encouraged by the find, divers were sent to the bottom.

After three days of examining the hulk, the divers found little more than metal fittings and iron spikes. Discouraged, leaders of the expedition were considering abandoning the project when a silver Spanish coin was found stuck to the bottom of one of the diver's boots. At last, claimed one of the leaders, the jinx had been broken. Another three weeks of searching, however, proved fruitless, and the Colstad Expedition disbanded.

During early spring of 1937, James Bartlett, a well-known ship captain, heard the tale of the sunken *deBraak* and its huge treasure for the first time, and related this interesting story: During the summer of 1907, Bartlett claimed, several gold ingots were found on the Lewes beach for several days following a severe storm. The ingots were far too heavy to have been carried to the shore by deep currents, so, Bartlett mused they were either buried at the location where they were found or they were part of the *deBraak*'s cargo where the ship actually went down. Because of the heavy deposition of sand on the beach during storms and the resulting extension of the coastline during the past one hundred and fifty years, Bartlett maintained that the hulk of the *deBraak* was actually buried under several feet of sand somewhere on the present beach. Very few people took Bartlett's notion seriously, but then in 1945, several more golden ingots were dug up on the Lewes beach.

In 1966, the D&D Salvage Company from Philadelphia applied for and received a permit from the state of Delaware to attempt a recovery of the *deBraak*'s treasure. Work got under way soon afterward, and several months later the salvage company's owners announced they had discovered the wreck. The *deBraak*, they explained, was half buried in sand and about seventy-five feet of water. To retrieve the treasure, they intended to dig the bottom sands from around the ship and attempt to lift it to the surface using a technique successfully employed by Swedish salvers when they raised a three hundred and thirty-year-old Viking ship discovered in Stockholm Harbor.

Though the D&D team worked through December 1967, they were unable to keep the swirling sediments of Delaware Bay from filling in every excavation they made. Finally, after exhausting their operating funds, the corporation returned to Philadelphia.

The jinx, according to the owners of the D&D Salvage Company, was responsible for the failure.

Historical records pertaining to the *deBraak* are impressively complete. It is an established fact that the ship was transporting a rich cargo of gold and silver coins, ingots, and jewels when it sank in Delaware Bay in 1798. Since then, though the *deBraak*'s wreck has been located several times, every attempt to retrieve the treasure has met with misfortune.

Many people don't believe in jinxes, but researchers who have studied the *deBraak*'s fate and its rich cargo remain puzzled at the curious string of bad luck associated with this vessel and its treasure.

The Mysterious Cargo
of the *Faithful Steward*

For years, vacationers, beachcombers, and treasure hunters alike have been finding two-hundred-year-old British and Spanish coins washed upon the beach located on the seaward side of a Delaware barrier island. The coins are believed to be part of a large shipment carried by the *Faithful Steward*, a British passenger ship bound for Philadelphia that sank a short distance offshore during a violent storm.

The *Faithful Steward* departed Londonderry, Ireland, in August 1785, with two hundred and forty-nine passengers and twenty-four crew members. In the ship's hold was a cargo of goods bound for the American settlements along with several kegs of coins. A large number of the coins, which consisted of British half-pences, were to be used for the American settlements. More coins, all packed tightly into wooden nail kegs, consisted of gold and silver Spanish specie. Why these Spanish denominations were part of the *Faithful Steward* shipment still remains a mystery.

Having considerable difficulty navigating through the dense fog that had settled along the Atlantic seaboard, the *Steward*, hoping to dock in Philadelphia, became lost and was approaching the southern Delaware coast, nearly one hundred miles southwest of the intended destination. With visibility near zero, the *Steward*'s captain was concerned that he might be dangerously close to land and decided to take a sounding. To his surprise, he found his ship was sailing in only twenty-five feet of water. As he shouted orders for his crewmen to turn the vessel, the *Steward* ran aground and became lodged in the bottom sand.

At dawn of the following day, September 2, the ship, despite the captain's and crew's efforts, was still stuck solidly in the sand. The captain noted then that his location was a short distance from the long barrier island that separated the Atlantic Ocean from Delaware's Indian River Bay. As passengers milled about the deck, the crew remained busy attempting to extricate the vessel from its predicament. No progress had been made by sunset, and the captain grew concerned when he noticed an approaching storm.

Within the hour, a strong gale struck the Delaware coast, and violent winds shook the hopelessly stranded *Steward* so forcefully that the ship began to break into pieces. Fighting the strong winds, the crew experienced great difficulty lowering the lifeboats into the water. When the passengers were finally loaded into the boats, they were rowed in the driving rain to the barrier island, eventually landing at a point now known as Delaware Seashore State Park. As the drenched passengers stood on the dark shore, they stared out into the surging waters and watched as the *Steward* was torn apart by waves and wind.

Rescuers arrived around midday on September 3, and saw trunks, masts, rigging, and other flotsam, along with several bodies, washing up onto the shore. A few of the passengers and crew searched among the debris for their belongings, but most of the *Steward*'s contents were lost in the shallow water about one hundred yards offshore.

Subsequent storms in this region during the following weeks served to further destroy what was left of the *Steward*'s deck and hull, and researchers and salvers claim nothing is left of the ship today. The kegs that transported the coins are believed to have sunk into the sand or shattered, releasing their contents upon the gently sloping continental shelf. Over the years, strong currents have carried many of the coins shoreward, and hundreds of half-pences and a lesser number of Spanish *reales* have been found along the barrier island beach from the town of Indian Beach south to Cottonpatch Hill. Area residents often refer to the region as "Coin Beach."

While the beaches may be rich with coins from the wreck of the *Faithful Steward*, the shallow waters about one hundred yards out into the Atlantic are even richer. In 1972, a diver found hundreds of British half-pence coins along with dozens of Spanish *reales* in one week's time. Others searching in about twelve to fifteen feet of water have also made impressive discoveries.

It is believed by most that thousands of the coins once transported by the *Faithful Steward* now lie scattered along the ocean bottom—from the shoreline out to approximately one hundred yards or more and extending for several miles up and down the barrier island coast.

MARYLAND

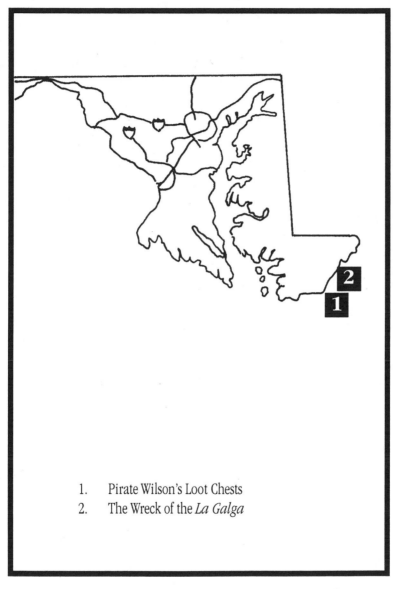

Pirate Wilson's Loot Chests

The notorious pirate Charles Wilson was well-known and greatly feared for years in ports and communities up and down the Atlantic seaboard as a result of his travels, exploits, and raids. His fate at the hands of a London executioner is also a matter of public record, but less well known about Wilson is a tale of an enormous treasure that he once buried on Assateague Island not long before his capture. The treasure, consisting of ten wooden chests filled with gold, silver, diamonds, and other jewels like rubies and emeralds, has eluded treasure hunters to this day.

As a pirate, Wilson enjoyed a career comparable to other notorious brigands of the day, but he maintained a low profile and preferred to remain anonymous. He believed, and rightly so, that his more flamboyant peers attracted far too much attention from those who would abolish raiding and pillaging on the high seas. Despite his efforts, Wilson was finally captured and sent to England to stand trial. There, he was found guilty of numerous crimes and sentenced to hang. America's Atlantic Coast residents, many who were Wilson's victims at one time or another, breathed a collective sigh of relief.

What remained unknown for nearly two hundred years after Wilson's execution was some amazing information about a tremendous fortune that he buried on Maryland's Assateague Island.

While awaiting the hangman in a London prison cell, Wilson wrote a letter to his brother, George, who still lived in Charleston, South Carolina. The letter, confiscated from Wilson just before his execution, was filed among stacks of official documents and remained lost for one hundred and ninety-eight years. It was finally discovered in 1948 and made public. It read:

The Year 1750
London, England

To my Brother, George Wilson,

There are three creeks lying 100 paces or more north of the second inlet above Chincoteague Island, which is at the south end of the peninsula. At the head of the third creek to the northward is a bluff facing the Atlantic Ocean with three cedar trees growing on it, each about one and one-third yards apart. Between the trees I buried ten iron-bound chests, bars of silver, gold, diamonds, and jewels to the sum of 200,000 sterling. Go to the woody knoll and remove the treasure.

The peninsula identified in Wilson's letter is Assateague Island. As soon as Wilson's long lost letter was printed in newspapers throughout England and America, a great rush of treasure hunters flocked to the island trying to locate and retrieve the pirate's buried treasure. None were successful, however, for during the nearly two centuries since Wilson buried his fortune, the incessant work of time and weather had changed the island's geographic configuration.

Since Wilson's last trip to the barrier island, as many as eleven new inlets had been cut through Assateague—some by man, others by nature. A few of the inlets used during Wilson's time had dried up and were now impassable. The trees identified in the letter had either been cut down or simply died and rotted away. In addition, because of the continual erosion and sand deposition carried by ocean currents and storm waves, Assateague Island, according to geographers, has actually migrated slowly westward. Portions of the island that existed several feet above the shoreline two hundred years ago are now underwater and exposed only at low tide.

Assateague Island, a long barrier island best known for its herds of tiny wild ponies, extends along the Atlantic Coast from Ocean City, Maryland, in a south-southwesterly direction to a point east of Wallops Island, Virginia. The northern three-fourths of the island belongs to the state of Maryland, the southern one-fourth to Virginia. Initial efforts to locate and retrieve Wilson's buried treasure during the 1950s were confined to the Virginia portion of the barrier island, but close examination of historical and contemporary maps, along with a studied reading of the pirate's last letter, has led most researchers to conclude that the chests of gold, silver, and jewels were buried somewhere just north of the Maryland-Virginia border and close to the island's eastern shore. Many firmly believe that the cache site is now under water.

During the 1960s, a young enlisted man was assigned to the Assateague Island Coast Guard Station. One day while walking along the sandy beach, he discovered a handful of sand-encrusted, colored stones that he placed in his pocket. Later, he washed the sandy coating from the stones and discovered they were of a bright red color and almost glasslike in appearance. Weeks passed, and the guardsman gave one of the stones, a particularly attractive one and as big around as a twenty-five cent piece, to his mother. She admired it very much and placed it upon the mantlepiece. A few weeks passed, and the mother, on a hunch, took the pretty red stone to a jeweler who immediately identified it as a ruby. When the mother told her son the stone's value, he went searching for the place where he first found the ruby. The son spent hours looking for the spot but never located it.

Though the Coast Guard station is located several miles south of the presumed location of Wilson's buried cache, searchers believe that the wooden chests holding the treasure have rotted away, leaving the booty scattered along the ocean floor and at the mercy of waves and currents. In this manner, with the area's prevailing currents, some of the precious stones could have been effectively carried along and deposited upon Assateague Island's sandy beaches for miles.

Because Wilson's buried treasure on Assateague Island is currently estimated to be worth more than $10 million renewed interest in the site has been expressed by a number of professional treasure hunting consortiums, and at least six organized searches have occurred since 1990. Thus far, however, there has been no report of discovery.

Historians who have studied Wilson's letter conclude the document is authentic. It has also been established that the pirate did, in fact, accumulate an incredible amount of treasure during his piracy days. Thus, the possibility that a huge pirate treasure is buried on Assateague Island is great.

The chances of finding it, however, may not be.

The Wreck of the *La Galga*

Desperately fighting its way through a hurricane, the Spanish galleon *La Galga* barely survived the raging seas and high winds along the North Carolina and Virginia coasts. Luck ran out on the vessel, however, just as it reached a point off the southern tip of Maryland. The *La Galga* finally succumbed to the violent storm and sank to the bottom of the Atlantic Ocean. In its hull, the galleon carried a huge treasure in gold coins and bullion bound for Spain. To this day, coins from the wreck of the *La Galga* have been found on Maryland beaches, but the sunken ship's location, apparently only a few hundred yards offshore, has never been identified.

In May 1750, a fleet of ten Spanish ships clogged the quiet and peaceful Havana, Cuba, harbor. The vessels, recently arrived from South American and Mexican ports, remained anchored in the bay for weeks as they were subjected to repairs, loaded with provisions, and readied for the long voyage across the Atlantic Ocean to Spain. Each year, the ships arrived in Havana around this time to make preparations for the journey and take advantage of the favorable winds that blew between May and July before the dreaded hurricane season struck. It was crucial that the ships arrive safely at the Spanish port of Cadiz because each one of them transported a fortune in gold for the country's treasury.

Annually, the Spanish carried great amounts of gold ore, bullion, and coins taken from the hundreds of mines operated throughout Mexico and South America to the motherland. These mines worked Indian slaves and yielded millions and millions of dollars in precious metal.

For ample reason, the sailors and officers who participated in the annual Spanish *flota* feared the moody Atlantic Ocean and were anxious to make the necessary repairs, lay in stores, and get underway. A delay increased the potential of facing the fury of the ocean's storms, and many of them recalled stories of disasters that befell the fleets of 1715 and 1733, which claimed the lives of thousands of their countrymen and the loss of millions in gold.

The entire Spanish fleet of 1715 was destroyed along the Florida coast and millions in gold was lost because of a terrible hurricane. The remains of the 1733 fleet also never made it beyond Florida, and the hulks of its wrecked ships as well as the cargoes of gold remain scattered along the sea floor.

While anchored in the Havana harbor, the 1750 fleet suffered one delay after another as repairs and maintenance progressed slowly. When the ships were finally declared seaworthy, it was well into August and dangerously close to hurricane season. Leaving Havana harbor, the ten ships sailed through the Florida Straits and northward into the open Atlantic Ocean toward the more favorable winds of the higher latitudes. All the while, crewmen glanced fearfully toward the sky and constantly scanned the horizons for any sign of an oncoming storm.

By the time the fleet reached a point opposite northern Florida, a hurricane struck and one of the ships sank immediately. Struggling against the fierce winds and high waves, the remaining nine vessels managed to sail almost to Cape Hatteras, North Carolina, approximately five hundred miles away, when four more were lost. The storm apparently carried the ships along with its winds and refused to allow them to escape.

The five remaining vessels continued northward with their masts and sails suffering severe damage along the way. Two of them, the *Nuestra Senora de Guadalupe* and the *Zumaca*, managed to reach the relative shelter of Chesapeake Bay and dropped anchor in Norfolk Bay. Two other ships wrecked upon the eastern shore of the peninsula that separates Chesapeake Bay from the Atlantic Ocean. The last vessel, the *La Galga*, finally went down somewhere off Assateague Island just north of the Maryland-Virginia border.

Amazingly, there were several survivors. After the *La Galga* sank, two dozen crewmen managed to swim or float to Assateague Island's eastern shore. After resting from their ordeal, they crossed Assateague, swam the bay separating the barrier island from the mainland, and finally arrived at a small inland settlement called Snow Hill, where they related the fate of the *La Galga*.

Today, the *La Galga* has attracted the interest of dozens of treasure hunters, who, collectively, have invested well over $1 million in salvage and recovery research and preparation. The reason for this interest is related to the fact that, in recent years, dozens of Spanish coins have been found washed up along Assateague Island following Atlantic storms. Investigators and collectors maintain the coins came from the cargo of the *La Galga*.

Researchers have estimated that the value of the gold carried by the *La Galga* would be worth between $40 to $50 million today.

VIRGINIA

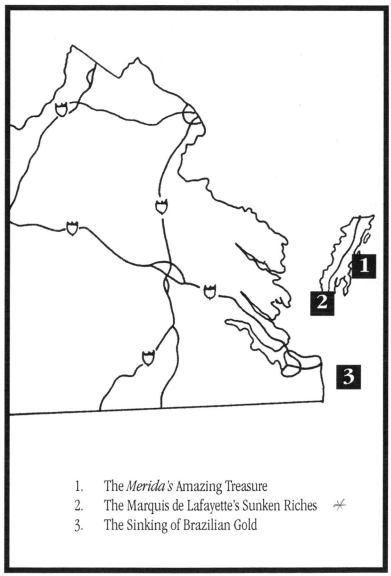

The *Merida's* Amazing Treasure

On May 8, 1911, the Merida sailed out of the Veracruz port in Mexico, carrying three hundred and thirty passengers, crew, and officers. A large amount of silver, seventeen tons to be exact, that was being transferred from unstable Mexican banks to United States repositories was also on the steamship. In addition, it was reported that the ship carried an estimated $500,000 worth of gold, four hundred and seventy tons of copper, a shipment of mahogany logs, six thousand tons of Jamaican rum, and several small chests filled with precious stones allegedly belonging to Emperor Maximilian.

The Merida, owned by the New York and Cuba Steamship Company, was four hundred feet long with steel bulkhead construction. With three decks, fore and aft, and boasting two huge steam engines capable of generating five thousand horsepower, the ship was a favorite of travelers from New York to Havana and back since she could complete the trip in seventy-two hours.

A few minutes after midnight on May 12, the Merida maintained its northward course and was only about ten hours from New York. Her route, unfortunately, took her through a dense fog about fifty miles off the Virginia coast.

The Admiral Farragut, a 291-foot long steamship from Philadelphia, sailed near the Merida. The Farragut, on a southward course bound for Kingston, Jamaica, traveled in the same shipping lane as the Merida. Both ships cruised at approximately fifteen knots. The two vessels, each unaware of the other, were on a fatal course.

At half past midnight, Merida crewmen spotted the lights of the Farragut that suddenly appeared off the bow and sounded the foghorn. Seconds later, as the Merida attempted to veer out of the path of the oncoming vessel, the two ships collided. The Farragut's steel bow rammed almost fifteen feet into the middle of the Merida. Almost immediately, the Merida with a gaping hole in the starboard plates and bulkheads took on water at an alarming rate.

As the Merida gradually sank lower into the Atlantic Ocean, the passengers were quickly and efficiently removed and transferred to the Farragut. Throughout the darkness of the early morning, the Merida remained afloat, but at 5:30 A.M. the stern raised almost perpendicular and the vessel disappeared into the dark waters.

By eight o'clock, the Merida's passengers were all accounted for, and the U.S.S. Iowa was escorting the Admiral Farragut to the New York harbor.

The sinking of the Merida became front page news in the United States for several days, but the event soon faded from public interest. About two weeks later, however, reports of the great fortune in silver and other valuable cargo carried aboard the vessel were leaked to the press and subsequent headlines brought renewed attention to the sunken Merida.

Within a few days, several teams of salvage operators were exploring the waters fifty miles off the coast of Virginia for the wreck of the Merida. According to the captain's log of the Admiral Farragut, the ship went down at latitude thirty-seven to twenty north, seventy-four to forty-seven west, forty-five miles east of Virginia's Cobb Island and in approximately two hundred feet of water.

In August 1911, Captain Charles Williamson, a noted Virginia salvor, announced that he would employ a newly patented submarine tube caisson in the first organized effort to recover the Merida's treasure. The caisson was a three-foot wide steel reenforced airtight tube attached to a large turret at the bottom and a salvage ship above the tube. Air was to be continuously pumped into the tube while men were working in it. Salvers would descend to the turret through the tube by way of a ladder. Once at the bottom, they had the capability of manipulating mechanical arms and claws to conduct the actual recovery.

From the beginning, Williamson's elaborate invention experienced mechanical and engineering problems compounded by heavy seas agitated by storms. After three weeks, Williamson abandoned the project.

In 1917, a second recovery attempt backed by several prominent New York businessmen was attempted. A trawler was contracted to drag the ocean in the area where the Merida went down. The ill-conceived and poorly executed salvage operation had little chance of success from the start, and stormy seas eventually caused the trawler to withdraw from the area.

In 1921, a salvage crew of around thirty men arrived in the Atlantic waters in the area of the Merida but were unable to locate the wreck.

The next expedition to try to locate and retrieve the treasure was organized in 1924 and headed by yet another group of wealthy New York businessmen who hired famous salvage diver Frank Grilley to manage the attempt. Grilley contracted two salvage trawlers, each with a crew of thirty men, and hired several noted former navy divers. Bad weather jeopardized the search from the start, and even with substantial funding and experienced divers, the group failed to retrieve anything of value from the sunken vessel. In late November, the expedition pulled out with plans to try again the following year.

Returning to the *Merida* on June 30, 1925, expedition divers located the sunken wreck during one of the initial reconnaissance dives. Using blueprints of the vessel, they identified a portion of the hull close to where the treasure was believed to be stored. To reach the treasure, however, it would be necessary to cut through the ship's thick steel.

As the salvors lowered cutting-torches to the wreck, a severe storm closed in on the region from the east, and officials in charge of the operation deemed it necessary to return to shore. Before leaving they set out marker buoys, but when they returned three days later, they discovered the buoys had been swept away by the storm, and they were unable to relocate the sunken ship.

During the 1930s, several more salvage companies announced plans to try and recover the *Merida*'s treasure. At the same time, a number of the original passengers in 1911, along with heirs of deceased passengers, filed claims on various amounts of the unre-covered treasure. Courtrooms were soon filled with claims, and all salvage operations were halted pending the results of litigation. The courts requested the United States Coast Guard send a cutter to the Atlantic Ocean and maintain a guard over the *Merida* to prevent rival salvors from trying to reach the treasure.

Following court deliberations, several attempts were made to penetrate the *Merida*'s steel hull but none were successful. At least a dozen salvage attempts were made between 1936 and 1939, but each one experienced serious problems with equipment failure and severe weather and were forced to give up the search without recovering anything.

World War II forced a halt to any organized searches for the *Merida* treasure, and no further attempts to reach it were under-taken until 1957 when several tons of copper bars were located and recovered. Though the recovery team succeeded in penetrating the thick hull of the wreck, the silver ingots eluded them.

During the 1960s and 1970s, as scuba gear became more available, several divers visited the wreck but all reported that they were unable to enter it. In 1972, a diver reported that the hull had been severely damaged by previous salvage attempts and ocean water corrosion, rendering it quite unsafe.

Today, several professional salvors claim to have located the *Merida* but state that large portions of the steel hull have collapsed inward and that most of the ship is buried in as much as twenty feet of sand. Experienced salvors estimate it would take well over one million dollars to finance a recovery of the treasure worth more than thirteen million dollars today, that is still believed to be inside the wreck of the *Merida*.

The Marquis de Lafayette's Sunken Riches

The mid-August heat of 1778 was uncomfortable for the thirteen men hiding in a thick grove of trees on Virginia's Smith Island. For days, they had awaited the arrival of the French vessel *Dupre*, so it was frustration and anger that they experienced as they watched helplessly as a British flotilla consisting of six warships attacked and sank the ship. The *Dupre* carried an estimated $50,000 in gold coin and bullion, funds desperately needed for the support of the American cause in the war for independence. Led by the notorious Marquis de Lafayette, the men on Smith Island could do little but watch the *Dupre*, badly shattered by the continuous bombardment from the British ships, sink beneath the waves carrying men and gold to the bottom of the Atlantic floor.

The Marquis de Lafayette became an important figure during the American Revolution. Born in France, Marie Joseph Paul Yves Roch Gilbert du Motier, as he was known in his early life, descended from French aristocracy. After serving for a short time in the French army, Lafayette traveled to America at the age of twenty to fight in support of the colonial ideals. He met George Washington, who grew to respect and admire the idealistic and fearless Frenchman. Lafayette, in turn, was impressed with Washington's courage and leadership, and the two forged a strong bond.

In a relatively short time, the Continental Congress awarded Lafayette the rank of major general. A firm believer in the

American ideals, Lafayette, in turn, worked very hard to secure financing from the French government to be used to support the war effort. During this time, the colonials were running short of supplies and ammunition and were desperate for support. At the same time, however, French political officials were reluctant to become deeply involved in American affairs because it feared British reprisal.

Following France's denial of funding, Lafayette turned to several prominent French businessmen known to secretly support the Americans. On the condition that they remain anonymous, the businessmen agreed to raise money and supplies and ship them to the colonies.

Approximately $50,000 in gold coin and bullion, along with ammunition and other important supplies obtained in Europe, were secretly loaded aboard several French merchant vessels. The vessels, all bound for the French West Indies in the Caribbean Sea, transferred their war cargo to the French frigate *Dupre*, a private vessel owned by Jean-Pierre Clement, a friend of Lafayette, who sought new business opportunities in the growing American colonies.

In July 1778, the *Dupre*, loaded with gold, ammunition, and war supplies, sailed from the West Indies for America. French merchant ships were common in Atlantic waters during this time, but British warships, ever wary of the increase in smuggling of essential goods to the Americans, had orders to fire upon suspect vessels. After sailing far to the north of the British-held Bahama Islands, the *Dupre* finally sighted the American coast around North Carolina. Always on the lookout for hostile ships, the French vessel followed the coastline northward to its predetermined Virginia destination, Smith Island, one of many islets east of the long, narrow peninsula that separates the Atlantic Ocean from the Chesapeake Bay.

Months earlier, Lafayette arranged for the *Dupre* to anchor just off Smith Island in the Atlantic waters so its cargo could be transferred into longboats. Given the fact that dozens of British men-o'-war patrolled the Atlantic Coast, it was with an incredible amount of luck that the *Dupre* managed to travel as far as it did without being sighted. Several days earlier, Lafayette, along with a dozen hand-picked men, rowed to Smith Island to wait for the *Dupre*. After pulling their boats into the concealment of a dense stand of trees about one hundred yards from the shoreline, the soldiers waited for days in hiding for the *Dupre*'s arrival. Once the French vessel was safely anchored offshore, Lafayette and his men intended to row out to the ship, transfer the gold and other cargo into the longboats, and return to some unnamed Virginia location.

Around mid-morning one day in August, a lookout alerted Lafayette that a French ship was approaching the island. With two companions, the Frenchman walked to the water's edge to signal the *Dupre*.

Suddenly, rounding the northern end of Smith Island, six British warships appeared, all of them bearing down on the *Dupre*. The crew of the *Dupre* was distracted with lowering the mainsail, and when the British ships were finally spotted, it was too late to prepare for battle. Realizing the impossibility of fleeing, the *Dupre*'s captain tried desperately to rally his seamen.

The *Dupre* was no match for the British attackers. The English warships were highly maneuverable, fast, and staffed with experienced officers and fighters as well as superior armament. As soon as they were within range of the *Dupre*, they attacked it ferociously with a deafening bombardment from dozens of cannons with the intention of sending it to the bottom of the ocean. Completely helpless, Lafayette and his men could only watch from the Smith Island shore as the *Dupre*, shattered and splintered from the constant cannon fire, slowly listed to one side and sank. As the stern of the French ship disappeared beneath the waves, Lafayette cursed his bad fortune at having lost the $50,000 in gold along with the important supplies.

Ill-equipped for recovering the sunken gold, Lafayette could do little but remain in hiding on Smith Island until the British ships sailed away. On the following morning, he ordered his men to pull the rowboats into the water and, after making certain they were not observed, journeyed to an assigned rendezvous somewhere on the Virginia coast. Though this mission was a failure, Lafayette went on to distinguish himself in many ways during the remainder of the American Revolution and succeeded on several other occasions in obtaining war funding from French businessmen.

Because of the ongoing war, no immediate attempt was made to recover the sunken gold. As months passed and the war effort continued demanding the attention of military and political leaders, the matter of the sunken *Dupre* and its cargo were soon forgotten.

Today, no record exists of any attempt whatsoever to recover the lost gold from the wreck of the *Dupre*. In fact, the exact location where the French frigate went down has been debated for well over one hundred years. Some claim its remains rest near the southern end of Smith Island, others maintain the ship was sunk closer to the northern shore.

$50,000 worth of gold at 1778 values carry a considerably greater value today, perhaps over $1 million and the antique and artifact value alone could possibly command higher prices. It is likely that most of the *Dupre* has rotted away on the Atlantic floor not far from Smith Island during the past two centuries. The gold, however, though probably badly corroded, is still there, perhaps scattered about the ocean floor.

Interest in the *Dupre* and its gold shipment was rekindled in 1991 when a beachcomber discovered a French gold coin with a 1777 mint date on the eastern shore of Smith Island following a storm.

The Sinking of Brazilian Gold

On a stormy August night in 1908, the captain of the Dutch ore freighter, the *Edwijk*, pondered an important decision. As the ore ship fought the heavy seas during a violent storm off the North Carolina coast, the captain pulled closer and closer to the shoreline where the waves were less intense. For a time, he considered seeking shelter among the many small islets near the coast, but he feared running the heavy ship aground. Determined he would rather fight his way through the storm, the captain turned the *Edwijk* into the wind. After the freighter passed False Cape near the southeastern tip of Virginia, the storm increased in intensity and tossed the heavy vessel about as if it were no more substantial than a tiny rowboat. Desperate, the captain transmitted an emergency message concerning his predicament to a contact in Norfolk. As he spoke into his microphone, huge waves smacked against the freighter's hull, and the ship quickly took on water. The captain soon reported that the *Edwijk* was sinking and requested a rescue. A few seconds later, however, all radio contact ceased, and the *Edwijk* was never heard from again. In an estimated one hundred forty feet of water, the Dutch ship, carrying well over one million dollars' worth of Brazilian gold, sank to the floor of the Atlantic Ocean.

Since European explorers arrived in South America during the sixteenth century, the rich gold fields that they discovered in Brazil were spoken of with a kind of hushed reverence throughout much of the civilized world. Within a few short years, the Brazilian gold harvests became almost legendary, and Portuguese fleets crossed and recrossed the Atlantic Ocean carrying gold bullion, nuggets, and dust to that country's growing treasury.

Because of a variety of political and logistical problems, the Brazilian gold fields became neglected for a number of decades, but in 1908, a group of European entrepreneurs formed the Middle Atlantic Mining Consortium to finance the reopening of several abandoned mines in the southeastern part of Brazil. As impressive amounts of gold were mined from the old shafts, the consortium reinvested some of their profit into the exploration and prospecting for several new mining locations, and within a short time, several more extraordinary discoveries were made. During the ensuing months, just over one million dollars' worth of high-grade gold bullion was ready for shipment.

Since the earliest discovery of gold by the consortium, disagreements among the members led to the filing of several lawsuits and numerous attempts to dissolve the company. Consequently, the ownership of the gold bullion remained unclear. To further complicate matters, legal considerations determined that the gold needed to be removed from Brazil as soon as possible. Subsequent disagreements erupted relative to where it should be taken. Because members of the consortium consisted of citizens of France, Belgium, England, and Switzerland, it was finally agreed that the gold be temporarily stored in a neutral country—the United States.

In August 1908, the gold ingots were loaded aboard the Edwijk, an independently owned four-masted schooner registered in the Netherlands, also a neutral country.

With the gold and a hull filled with other cargo, the overloaded Edwijk sailed out of the Rio de Janeiro port and made its way northward toward its ultimate destination—New York Harbor.

The journey into and through the Caribbean Sea was uneventful, and the freighter finally came in sight of the Florida coast.

As the *Edwijk* passed Florida and continued on its way parallel to the Georgia coastline, a huge storm was building in the Atlantic several miles off the New York coast. By the time the *Edwijk* reached Cape Hatteras in North Carolina, the skies had darkened perceptibly and the winds had increased. After leaving Cape Hatteras, the freighter proceeded cautiously along the coast toward Virginia.

As the *Edwijk* neared the North Carolina-Virginia border, the storm had increased to the degree that the ship's captain debated turning around and seeking shelter among North Carolina's barrier islands, but having successively endured rough seas in the past, he finally decided to continue on course, hoping the storm would soon abate.

By the time the *Edwijk* arrived at some point a mile or two off False Cape, the storm had intensified and control of the huge freighter was no longer possible. As crewmen struggled to lower the sails, others fought with the rudder, trying to face into the gale.

The option of sailing into the shelter of the coastal islands once again occurred to the *Edwijk*'s captain, but he feared the overloaded vessel would run aground. The ship's hull soon began breaking apart as a result of the severe storm, and at this point the captain attempted to radio for help. Radio contact was finally made with a station in nearby Norfolk, and as men listened, the *Edwijk*'s captain screamed for help and stated that the ship was sinking. Seconds later, the communication ended.

The next day, several rescue ships cruised the area off False Cape in search of survivors, but debris from the wrecked *Edwijk* was all that was found. No one has ever ascertained precisely where the freighter went down, and salvage attempts have been frustrating because this portion of the Atlantic Ocean is littered with hundreds of shipwrecks.

The members of the Middle Atlantic Mining Consortium settled their differences and reinvested in several more Brazilian gold mining efforts. Initially, the members were prepared to finance a salvage attempt and retrieve the gold aboard the *Edwijk*, but following several new and profitable ore discoveries, they eventually abandoned the recovery project and concentrated their efforts and resources on mining activities.

Since then, only a few ill-equipped and poorly organized attempts have been made to locate the wreck of the *Edwijk*, but no success was ever reported.

NORTH CAROLINA

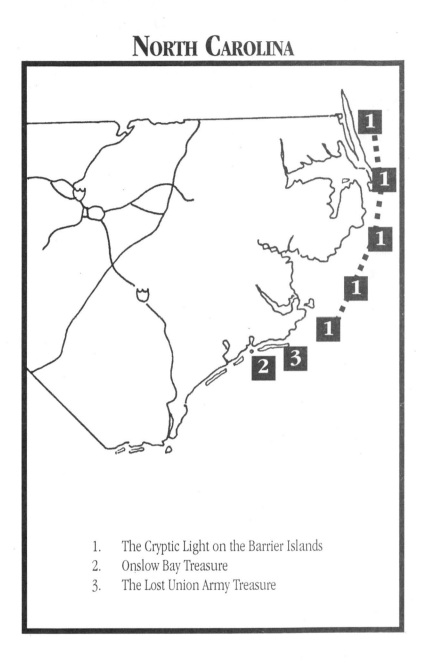

The Cryptic Light
on the Barrier Islands

The town of Nags Head, North Carolina, is a barrier island community of some two thousand people. During the early 1800s, however, this region was sparsely populated save for a few area fishermen and the residents of tiny villages along the coast. During severe storms, sailing vessels often sought refuge in the more shallow sounds and bays located between the barrier islands and the mainland along this stretch of the coast to avoid the dangerous waves and winds of the open sea.

One dark night, a poor fisherman made repairs on his leaky boat by lantern light. A heavy rain, preceding an ocean storm, began to fall, and the fisherman hurried about his task in the hope of completing it before the storm arrived.

Two-and-a-half miles out to sea, a merchant ship, anxious to find refuge in the face of the oncoming storm, spotted the light from the fisherman's lantern. Mistakenly believing it was the light from another ship on its way through an inlet into the sound, the merchant vessel started following it. In the darkening night, and with visibility considerably reduced as a result of the heavy rain, the lookout could not see the barrier island that the ship was approaching.

Moments later, the ship struck a shoal and went no further. After lowering lifeboats, the ship's officers and crew rowed the remaining few hundred yards to the island and were dismayed to discover the light they were following was the stationary lantern belonging to the fisherman. Cursing the poor fisherman and their own bad luck, the seamen continued on in the hope of securing a rescue for their ship.

Weeks later, as the story of the foundered ship was spread throughout the region, several unscrupulous bankers, desperate to add to their dwindling stocks of funds, met to devise a wicked scheme. In order to fill their coffers, they decided to attempt to lure potential treasure ships onto the treacherous shoals and loot the vessels of their cargoes.

Over the years, dozens of ships that ran aground just off the barrier island from Nag's Head north to Kitty Hawk are believed to have fallen victim to the bankers's trick. When the ship's crews would leave the stranded vessels in search of help, the bankers, with the aid of several hired men, would row out to the ships and remove the cargoes.

A typical victim was the *Florence*, a two-masted freighter traveling from Veracruz, Mexico, to England. In the *Florence*'s hold was $300,000 in gold ingots bound for the Bank of England.

After taking on supplies at the harbor in Charleston, South Carolina, the *Florence* set sail for higher latitudes before attempting an Atlantic crossing. On passing Cape Hatteras, the *Florence* encountered a storm and the captain decided against sailing into it. Instead, he searched for an inlet that would lead him to the relative safety of one of the sounds located behind the barrier island. With that in mind, the captain steered the ship closer to the coastline.

Awaiting on the barrier island, the bankers tied a ship's lamp around the horse's neck and led the animal up and down a portion of the beach, hoping to deceive the ship into thinking it was another boat. As the *Florence* approached Nag's Head, the lookout suddenly shouted that he had spotted a light in the distance that he identified as a ship's lamp. Knowing the *Florence* was quite close to the shore, the captain reasoned the ship in the distance had located an inlet and was entering it. With confidence, he ordered his helmsman to follow the light. Thirty minutes later, the *Florence* struck a shoal, capsized, and all thirty-one men aboard drowned.

The following morning after the storm had subsided, the bankers, along with their henchmen, rowed out to the *Florence*. By evening, the ingots, along with other cargo, had been removed from the wreck, carried to shore, and buried.

This scheme was so effective that it is estimated that millions of dollars' worth of gold and silver ingots and coins, jewelry, and other valuable objects were removed from the trapped ships. Eventually, ship captains learned about the false light and avoided the Nag's Head area thereafter.

After looting the foundered ships, the bankers buried the cargo at various locations along the beach, returning to them from time to time to extract some for their banks. The bankers and their henchmen were so successful obtaining treasure from the numerous wrecks that far more of it was eventually cached than they could keep track of. Because some of the caches were poorly marked or not marked at all, many of them were also lost. Heavy storms also often changed the topography of the shoreline and modified landmarks so that it was difficult to locate previously buried caches.

Eventually, the bankers moved on, but millions in gold and other items remained hidden on the beach near Nag's Head. As the years passed, the treasures buried on the barrier island beach were gradually forgotten.

In 1929, an engineer named Kindervater arrived at Nag's Head, near Kitty Hawk, to erect a granite memorial commemorating the Wright Brother's earliest airplane flight. After deciding on an

140

appropriate site, Kindervater supervised the excavation of a portion of the beach. During the process, engineer Kindervater was surprised to discover a number of valuable items apparently buried in the sand, including coins and an impressive silver punch bowl. More digging unearthed even more treasures!

When word of Kindervater's discoveries circulated, people came from miles away to dig in the beach sands from Kitty Hawk down to Nag's Head. In eighteen months time, more than a million dollars' worth of coins, ingots, jewelry, and other items were discovered, all believed to be among the loot taken from vessels lured aground years earlier.

Researchers believe that dozens of ships fell victim to the bankers' scheme and that millions of dollars in treasure were cached at various locations near Nag's Head. The researchers also note that much of the treasure remains today, perhaps to be uncovered in the future from another chance excavation or storm erosion.

Onslow Bay Treasure

The *Nettle*, a well-constructed barkentine built by expert British ship builders, served England for a number of years as a freighter. Many times, this sleek vessel plied the Atlantic waters from the British Isles to America and back, and once served as a trade ship along the African coast under the authority of the British East India Company.

James Christopher Patent, the *Nettle*'s captain, had commanded the ship since its maiden voyage, and was well-respected and admired among England's seamen. During the years of his appointment, Patent, a natural politician and businessman, cultivated many friends among British royalty, politicians, and businessmen. It was with little difficulty, therefore, that he was able to purchase the ship several years later in order to go into business for himself.

Patent was convinced he could make a fortune by converting the *Nettle* into a passenger ship. In 1851, he sailed the ship to America and established a thriving business ferrying goods, businessmen, and vacationers up and down the Atlantic Coast from the port of New York to Panama and points in between.

A west coast counterpart to the *Nettle* was the *Leilah*, a steam-powered vessel making a grand profit for its owners carrying passengers and freight up and down the west coasts of the United States, Mexico, and Central America. In April 1858, the *Leilah* steamed from San Francisco Bay carrying two hundred and fifty passengers, mostly miners and businessmen, along with $2 million in gold ingots. The ingots, stamped out in various mills in northern California, were destined for New York City where they would be unloaded and shipped to a federal mint. Many of the miners and businessmen who booked passage on the *Leilah* had recently quit the California gold fields and carried along their personal fortunes in gold nuggets and dust. Some allowed their gold to be locked in the ship's safe; others simply hid it in their staterooms.

The *Leilah* did not operate on the east coast, so on arriving at Panama City, its passengers disembarked and boarded the *Nettle* that lay at anchor nearby. The gold ingots were transferred from the *Leilah* and stacked in the hold of Captain Patent's vessel.

The *Nettle* was not as large as the *Leilah*, and the great weight of the gold caused Patent's vessel to ride quite low in the water. In addition, the two hundred fifty passengers who came aboard dangerously exceeded the ship's capacity, and as many as five men were forced to share the cramped quarters in each of the tiny staterooms. Grossly overloaded, the *Nettle* sailed out of the canal, into the Caribbean Sea, past the eastern end of Cuba, and northward through the Bahama Islands toward New York.

As the *Nettle* sailed past a point opposite Jacksonville, Florida, a violent tropical storm descended upon the region. Though the ship's crewmen fought valiantly, the billowing waves and vicious winds snapped the masts and carried away the sails. Moments later, the rudder broke, and the helpless *Nettle* blew northward under the power of the storm.

As the *Nettle* neared the North Carolina coast, the winds from the now diminishing storm took her toward the shore. Drifting into increasing shallow waters, the *Nettle* was not at the mercy of the sharply breaking waves. When the ship was approximately two to three miles southeast of Onslow Bay's Bear Inlet, a steep surging wave struck the ship broadside and capsized it.

Miraculously, nearly fifty men were able to scramble from their staterooms and cabins into the Atlantic and clutch desperately to the overturned boat's hull. The other passengers, more than two hundred of them, remained trapped in the overturned ship; Captain Patent was among them.

A nearby ship, the *Cormorant*, spotted the capsized *Nettle* through the diminishing rain and sped toward her. Less than thirty minutes after the survivors were pulled aboard, the *Nettle* plummeted downward toward the sea bottom, carrying its victims and an incredible fortune in gold with it.

Anxious to deliver the survivors to the nearest port, the captain of the *Cormorant* ordered the ship to proceed at all haste and only made vague notes relative to the location where the *Nettle* went down. As a result, subsequent salvage attempts have encountered difficulty in determining the precise location of the wreck and its cargo of gold.

Though many salvage companies and several professional treasure hunters have invested a great deal of time, energy, and money into searching for the sunken *Nettle*, the wreck's location has never been positively identified. The *Nettle's* gold ingots still lie untouched in the shifting sands of Onslow Bay's continental shelf. This treasure, along with the passengers' personal fortunes that were stored in the ships safe or hidden in staterooms, is easily worth more than $10 million today.

The Lost Union Army Treasure

Prior to the 1861 battle for the Confederate-held Fort Macon, Union troops assembled on a portion of the mainland coast now occupied by the present-day town of Morehead City, North Carolina. The low horizon of Bogue Bank, a narrow barrier island separating the Bogue Sound from the Atlantic Ocean, could be seen just south of the sound.

Fort Macon, the target for the Union assault only scant hours away, was on the eastern end of the island. Not far from where the Union soldiers stood near the shoreline, a treasure estimated to be worth tens of thousands of dollars was buried prior to their crossing the sound. Years later, the only man left alive who remembered where the treasure was buried died just before returning to it, and its location remains unknown to this day.

Fort Macon, overlooking a portion of the North Carolina coast, was originally constructed by the Federals. Both Yankees and Rebels regarded the small fort, which was generally occupied by less than twenty soldiers, as having strategic importance. Because of the reduced manpower, the Confederates quickly gained the fort in 1861 when Captain Josiah Pender, accompanied by a force of fifty troops, captured it. For more than a year, Pender's army remained in command of Fort Macon and kept their cannons pointed toward the open waters of the Atlantic Ocean ready to defend against an attack from a Union armada.

In April 1862, Union General Ambrose Burnside received orders to retake Fort Macon from the Confederates as soon as possible. Burnside was troubled somewhat by the assignment because none of the young soldiers in his company of two hundred charges had ever seen battle. He was concerned their lack of experience could jeopardize the operation. A shrewd military strategist, Burnside, however, decided to learn all he could about the fort and its occupants. So he sent his trusted scouts to the region to study the position of the bastion and the geography of the land. Meanwhile, Burnside subjected his young troopers to intensive training in preparation for the coming assault.

Several days later, Burnside learned from his scouts that Fort Macon was situated on the eastern end of a barrier island called Bogue Banks and separated from the mainland by about a mile of open water. The scouts also noted that all of the fort's cannons were pointed toward the ocean in anticipation of an attack from that direction. After thoroughly analyzing this situation, the general decided to launch a surprise attack on the fort from the rear. On the following morning, Burnside put several men to work constructing rafts stout enough to float cannons and troopers across the channel.

Early on the morning of the planned attack, Burnside's solders massed at the point of land where Morehead City now sits. While the general discussed last minute battle preparations with his lieutenants, Sergeant Gore, a thirty-five-year-old veteran of several skirmishes addressed the assembled soldiers. Walking among the rows and columns of soldiers, he instructed each one of them to remove rings, watches, jewelry, and money and place the items in a sack that was to be buried in a secret location just prior to departing for battle. The general, Gore informed the soldiers, did not want any valuables to fall into the hands of the Confederate soldiers. Actually, Burnside was not aware of Gore's devious plan.

When some of the troopers resisted turning over their valuables to the sergeant, Gore suggested they appoint one man that they could trust to accompany him to the secret location. They quickly elected Joseph Poindexter, a young private from Pennsylvania. Moments later Gore and Poindexter disappeared into the nearby woods and buried the heavy sack among the roots of a large cedar tree. It is estimated that several thousand dollars' worth of money and jewelry were cached.

A short time later, the rafts carrying men and cannons rowed toward Fort Macon. When they landed on the beach a short distance north of the fort, the men set up the cannons and a furious bombardment of the bastion began. When it appeared as though the Rebel defenders were significantly weakened, Burnside ordered his soldiers over the walls with instructions to kill or capture the Confederates.

During the ensuing fight inside the fort, dozens of men were killed, Confederate and Union soldiers alike. Eventually, however, the Rebels were forced to surrender and the fort once again fell into the hands of the Union forces.

While counting the dead, Union soldiers noted that Private Poindexter had been shot in the back of the head. Many of them believed Sergeant Gore had murdered the young trooper during the assault on the fort and suspected he intended to return alone to the buried treasure cache with the intention of retrieving the valuables for himself. No one, however, was willing to level a formal accusation at the sergeant.

As the soldiers debated among themselves about how to deal with the situation, Burnside's company suddenly received orders to return to the mainland and lend support to a Union company engaged in a fierce battle with Rebel soldiers several miles away. Following a hasty assembly, the troops, accompanied by Burnside, rowed back across the sound and headed inland. Sergeant Gore was given a command of ten soldiers and placed in charge of Fort

Macon. The following day, however, most of the troopers who accompanied Burnside were killed during the fighting.

Sergeant Gore remained at Fort Macon for the remainder of the Civil War. During the last few months of the war, the sergeant became very ill and often lapsed into fits of violent coughing. When the South finally surrendered in 1865, he decided the time was appropriate to return to the mainland and dig up the treasure he had cached four years earlier.

Weakened by his sickness, Gore asked a local fisherman to row him to the North Carolina shore. Gore and the fisherman had become friends during the preceding months and spent a great deal of time together drinking and playing cards. On the way to the mainland, Gore, in between fits of coughing, told the fisherman about the buried treasure and offered to split it with him.

As Gore was being rowed across the sound by his friend, he described the site where he buried the treasure three years earlier. He spoke of a large cedar tree not far from the shoreline with numerous thick exposed roots. The bag of treasure, he claimed, was buried only about eighteen inches deep.

When the rowboat skidded onto the beach, Gore attempted to climb out when he was seized by a sudden fit of coughing. After several minutes, he finally collapsed backward into the skiff. Concerned the ex-soldier could die before leading him to the location of the buried treasure, the fisherman carried Gore to a nearby doctor's home. After examining Gore, the doctor diagnosed him with typhoid fever. Gore never regained consciousness and died the following morning.

Several days later, the fisherman returned to the area where Gore claimed the treasure was buried. To his dismay, he encountered hundreds of large cedar trees and nothing in particular to distinguish one from the other. After digging around the bases of several of them and finding nothing, he gave up and eventually forgot about the treasure.

As far as it is known, the Union soldiers' bag of valuables buried by Sergeant Gore has never been recovered. The growth and expansion of Morehead City has undoubtedly accounted for a great deal of change in the surrounding environment, but many continue to maintain that not far from the shoreline located east of the city lies a small fortune in rings, watches, and other items from the Civil War era.

SOUTH CAROLINA

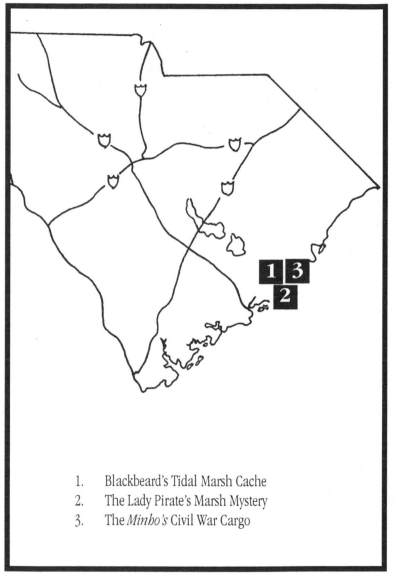

1. Blackbeard's Tidal Marsh Cache
2. The Lady Pirate's Marsh Mystery
3. The *Minho's* Civil War Cargo

Blackbeard's Tidal Marsh Cache

The pirate Blackbeard was rumored to have hidden treasure in many different locations. However, it is only known for certain that, on several occasions, he cached vast fortunes in gold and silver coins and ingots, along with chests stuffed with jewelry, in the tidal marshes near Charleston, South Carolina. Blackbeard never lived long enough to return for his Charleston treasure, and this great hoard, estimated to be worth nearly $100 million, remains lost.

Charleston, an Atlantic coastal town, is located on a point of land that extends between the Ashley and Cooper Rivers. Charles Towne, as it was originally called until 1783, was a bustling community that boasted one of the busiest ports on the Atlantic Coast. Almost daily, the Charles Towne port received great cargoes of sugar, rum, molasses, fruit, silk, and even precious stones. Here, these rich and varied cargoes were unloaded and brokered by local entrepreneurs. The future for the young city of Charles Towne as a trading and business center appeared prosperous.

The tidal marsh, a vast, swampy area, laid to the west of Charles Towne Bay. This marsh consisted of shallow water speckled with small islands of silt held together by clusters of densely growing vegetation. Charles Towne inhabitants generally avoided the marshes because they were hazardous to navigate and filled with aggressive mosquitoes and poisonous snakes. Quicksand was also an ever-present danger. For generations, stories about people entering the tidal marshes and never returning were numerous.

The first man known to have expressed a liking for the tidal marshes was Blackbeard. This notorious pirate took advantage of the forbidden nature of this hostile and primitive habitat to hide millions of dollars' worth of plunder gleaned from his numerous raids on merchant vessels throughout the Atlantic and Caribbean waters.

The swashbuckling brigand, who eventually became known to the world as Blackbeard, was born in England to a respectable family named Drummond. When he was about seventeen years old, young Drummond enlisted in the British navy under the name Edwin Teach. While serving in the navy, Drummond, also known as Teach, proved to be an able seaman and quickly learned the art and craft of sailing. By the time he was twenty years old, Teach was regarded as an expert on every aspect of sailing and maintaining ships.

Teach's lust for adventure and riches far exceeded the meager satisfaction he derived from serving as an apprentice seaman. Eventually, he left the navy, obtained his own ship, and began a long and successful career of piracy along the Atlantic Coast of America and in the Caribbean.

As years passed and Teach's fearsome reputation flourished, he adopted the name Blackbeard, a name derived from the thick, heavy, black beard that hung from his face and covered the upper part of his chest. Sometimes, the pirate would fasten ribbons of different colors to his beard, letting the long tails stream behind him in the blowing wind. Around his waist, Blackbeard wrapped colorful sashes into which he stuck knives, cutlasses, and pistols. Baggy silk trousers tucked into knee-high polished boots completed his outfit. Blackbeard looked quite unlike other pirates of his day.

In piracy, Blackbeard was fearless, ruthless, and bloodthirsty. He never manifested regret or remorse for his deeds, gave no quarter, and was known to vigorously kill men, women, and children. He never shied from battle and could be counted on to lead the attack on any ship that was overtaken and boarded. Sailors and crewmen aboard merchant vessels attacked by the pirate and his crew were known to leap into the sea rather than face Blackbeard's terrors.

Because of his charismatic flair and successes as a brigand, Blackbeard eventually commanded a large fleet of pirate vessels that preyed upon the merchant ships sailing the Caribbean and Atlantic. In this manner, and throughout his many years of terrorizing the waters, the colorful pirate accumulated a sizeable fortune in gold and silver bullion and coins along with several chests filled with jewels.

Following a series of successful raids, Blackbeard developed the habit of fleeing to the still waters of Charles Towne harbor to hide from pursuit.

Over the years, Charles Towne had become a favorite haunt of the pirate. He gradually fell in love with the location, the bay's calm waters, and the city's gentle people. Blackbeard also enjoyed the waterfront environment here, a place where he often caroused with fellow pirates and enjoyed the company of several women at a time. Though most of the Charles Towne citizens knew of Blackbeard and of the way he made his living, they amiably tolerated his presence, and perhaps even enjoyed the bit of notoriety he brought to the port settlement.

Eventually, Blackbeard purchased a fine house and several acres of Charles Towne land. Lavish hand-crafted furniture filled the house, and expensive silk curtains draped its windows. When not plundering ships and communities along the Atlantic Coast, Blackbeard enjoyed relaxing in his comfortable home.

Those who knew Blackbeard well realized the pirate favored the Charles Towne area for more practical reasons. Specifically, it was well known that Blackbeard was attracted to and even fascinated by the nearby tidal marshes. He regarded their near-impenetrable interior as the ideal place to hide the great amounts of treasure that he had accumulated over the years.

Sealing coins, ingots, and jewelry into wooden casks, Blackbeard, alone, would load them into a skiff, row out into the tidal marsh, and hide them in some pre-selected location. It is estimated that, at today's values, approximately $100 million worth of treasure was cached by the pirate in this forbidding and remote area.

In 1670, the government offered a general pardon to any and all pirates who agreed to give up raiding and return the items they had stolen. The offer of a pardon held great appeal for Blackbeard, who was gradually tiring of the pursuit by British and American forces. He also believed it was only a matter of time before he was eventually caught and killed. On the other hand, Blackbeard did not wish to give up the incredible fortune that he had accumulated over years of raiding and hidden in the tidal marsh.

Taking advantage of the opportunity for a pardon, and having great success in bribing a number of high government officials, Blackbeard was eventually forgiven for his piratical sins and settled down to a peaceful existence in Charles Towne. His treasure, hidden deep in the tidal marsh, was intact.

Now that he was an incredibly wealthy man no longer pursued by the authorities, Blackbeard gradually settled into a comfortable married life with a sixteen-year-old girl, and during the first few months of retirement, he even made plans to purchase a large plantation.

Blackbeard's commitment to a sedentary life did not last long. His lust for adventure and plunder was not easily quelled, and after a year of city living, the pirate began thinking about returning to the high seas. Unable to stand what he considered the ex-tremely restrictive and boring life of a "gentleman," Blackbeard finally reassembled his band of brigands and took to the oceans and piracy once again.

This time, however, Blackbeard was not so lucky. Not long after returning to piracy, his fleet fell into battle with two pursuing warships. Only moments after privateers had overtaken and boarded Blackbeard's vessel, the pirate, fighting valiantly, was shot and killed.

With Blackbeard's death went the knowledge of the location of his great pirate cache in Charles Towne's tidal marsh, a treasure which, from all accounts, is still there.

The Lady Pirate's Marsh Mystery

Charles Towne and the nearby tidal marshes appealed to someone other than Blackbeard. Mary Anne Townsend, the only successful female pirate on record, is also believed to have buried millions of dollars' worth of stolen booty in these treacherous South Carolina swamps. Pursued by the authorities, Townsend found it necessary to abandon her Charles Towne hideout and flee to South America. In her haste, however, she was forced to leave behind a tremendous treasure cache, which, according to record, has not been located to this day.

Mary Anne Townsend grew up in Jamestown, Virginia, the niece of a prominent and wealthy government official. Well-educated and frequently seen attending important society functions, the young and attractive Townsend was admired by many young men, but she possessed an adventurous streak she kept hidden from her relatives and peers.

While accompanying her uncle to Bermuda on a business trip one summer, Townsend encountered the notorious pirate Blackbeard. After her uncle had completed several important business transactions, he and Townsend were sailing out of Bermuda waters on the *Shropshire Lass* when it was suddenly attacked by Blackbeard and his cutthroats. Townsend watched in horror as the pirates, after boarding the defenseless passenger vessel, killed dozens of the crew and passengers. Horrified, yet oddly fascinated, Townsend watched as Blackbeard's ruffians beat and tied several men and women and forced them to walk the plank into the shark-infested waters.

When her turn arrived to climb aboard the plank, Townsend, with her hands securely tied behind her, squared her shoulders and spit into the faces of the dirty pirates, daring them to kill her. At just over six-feet tall with a statuesque build and long, flaming red hair, Townsend was an impressive sight. When one of the pirates prodded her toward the limit of the plank with a harpoon, she cursed him roundly and kicked him sharply, knocking him to the deck. Standing defiantly upon the plank, she berated the pirates, calling them cowards and daring them to touch her.

At this point, Blackbeard approached the plank and addressed Townsend for the first time. Her beauty, poise, and spirit immediately captivated him. Here, he thought, was a woman worth sparing, a woman worthy of famous fighting seaman such as himself. Stepping forward, he removed his hat and bowed deeply before Townsend, inviting her to step down from the plank and join him in his cabin.

Blackbeard was fascinated by Townsend. Uncharacteristically, he behaved graciously when she was nearby, and his followers talked quietly among themselves about the sudden and strange change in their leader's deportment. Eventually, Blackbeard began to court the striking woman.

Though the pirate leader would not allow Townsend to leave the ship, he provided her a comfortable room furnished with the finest of carved furniture and silk curtains. He employed a cook to prepare special meals only for her. He bestowed her with jewels, gold, silver, and fine cloth, all taken during his raids on area ships and coastal communities. Promising Townsend a life of wealth, luxury, and adventure, Blackbeard finally asked her to marry him.

This roguish man intrigued Townsend, but she was equally keen in exploring the promised opportunities for adventure. After giving his proposal several days of concentrated thought, Townsend finally agreed to wed the colorful brigand. Following a brief honeymoon, Townsend committed herself to a life of piracy and began accompanying her husband on his raiding forays.

Townsend readily adapted to the high seas lifestyle, relished the thought of capturing treasures and merchant ships, and begged Blackbeard to teach her all he knew. Happily, he tutored and encouraged the willing Townsend, and eventually the two made the most amazing pair of pirates ever to sail the oceans.

After a year of participating in a number of raids and seizures, Townsend, having proved herself almost as fearless and dangerous as her infamous husband, begged Blackbeard for a ship of her own to command. Always agreeable where she was concerned, Blackbeard provided her with the *Odyssey*, a swift vessel seized during an earlier attack.

By this time, Townsend had acquired a formidable reputation of her own and had little trouble assembling a competent crew of sailors and fighters. Within weeks, she was plundering ships throughout the Atlantic Ocean and Caribbean Sea with abandonment.

In addition to teaching Townsend all he knew about piracy, Blackbeard also introduced her to the wonders and pleasures of Charles Towne. Together, the two were often seen arm-in-arm going from tavern to tavern drinking ale and swapping tales with other freebooters.

Once, while in Charles Towne, Blackbeard told Townsend about hiding his treasures in a secret location deep in the tidal marsh and offered to show it to her. On several occasions, the two were seen rowing into the marsh, and many believe that Townsend is the only person who ever actually saw Blackbeard's incredible cache.

Eventually, Townsend herself selected a place deep in the marsh to hide her own accumulated treasure, and researchers estimate that over the years she added several million dollars' worth of booty, including ingots, coins, and jewelry.

Unlike Blackbeard, Townsend seldom entered the marshes alone. Instead, she generally employed two stout sailors to row two boatloads of treasure at a time to her hiding place. It was often rumored that, while Townsend and the two men were often observed entering the tidal marsh, she always returned alone.

During a long season of attacking merchant ships in the Caribbean Sea one year, Townsend received word that Blackbeard had been killed. Weeks later, on arriving at the Jamaican port in Kingston, she learned that a fleet of privateers had left the Carolina coast in pursuit of her and her cutthroats and were on their way to Jamaica. Townsend also discovered that a huge reward had been offered for her—dead or alive.

Fearing for her life, Townsend never returned to the United States. Instead, she immediately filled the hold of the Odyssey with provisions and set sail for South America where she believed she would be safe from pursuit and capture. The only treasure that she carried with her was what was currently stored in her ship's hold at the time. The booty cached in the Charles Towne tidal marshes in the location only Townsend knew remained hidden and untouched.

During the next decade, numerous tales circulated about this red-haired spitfire, but none have ever been verified. The most common related story was that she eventually arrived in Lima, Peru, and wed a wealthy Spanish landowner and businessman.

For years, residents of Charles Towne, well aware that Townsend had hidden a great treasure in the marsh, awaited for her to return and retrieve it. As the years passed, however, it became clear that would not happen, and the treasure was eventually forgotten.

Several forays into the tidal marsh some one hundred years following the disappearance of Townsend failed to locate any sign of the treasure. Many area residents are not aware of the cache's existence today, but those who know about it remain frustrated with the perils of the tidal march, considered by many to be as dangerous today as it was more than two centuries ago.

The hidden treasure of Mary Anne Townsend, as far as is known, still lies there.

The *Minho's* Civil War Cargo

Near midnight on October 21, 1862, the commercial ship *Minho* chugged slowly along the southern margin of Sullivans Island, a small barrier island located near the entrance to Charleston Harbor. For five months, the *Minho* had successfully penetrated blockades set up by Union ships and delivered its precious cargo to Southern customers.

The *Minho* did not carry ordinary cargo. Stored in the hull of the vessel were two hundred tons of rich transport including cases of imported wines, fine silks, expensive glass and china, and valuable medicines—all extremely rare since the beginning of the war. Wealthy Southerners, determined not to alter their lifestyles despite the ongoing war, paid high prices for these items transported by the *Minho*.

Unknown to many at the time, the *Minho* also carried a shipment of firearms destined for the Confederate army. Dozens of crates of Enfield rifles were stored in the hull in containers disguised as toolboxes.

The iron-hulled *Minho* was constructed in Scotland eight years earlier. At one hundred seventy-five feet long, a four hundred ton displacement, and a state-of-the-art steam propeller engine, the ship was fast and maneuverable, features deemed invaluable while running the Union blockades.

The *Minho* was eventually purchased by Fraiser, Trenholm, and Company, a shipping enterprise that owned a number of vessels that carried goods from Europe to America and back.

George Wigg, a representative of the shipping company, learned that wealthy landowners in the South were willing to pay premium prices for certain valuable and hard-to-obtain imported goods. Sensing a high-profit market, Wigg arranged to have a variety of such goods transported to Bermuda, loaded onto the *Minho*, and carried to selected American ports along the Atlantic Coast and sold to customers. The only obstacle, realized Wigg, was seizure by Federal ships that had been ordered to stop all shipments to Southern ports. The potential profit, Wigg convinced the company's owners, was worth the risk.

The *Minho*'s captain had previously delivered goods to the port of Charleston and was quite familiar with the harbor. After arriving from an easterly direction, he planned to navigate the vessel along the southern margin of Sullivans Island until arriving at the harbor's entrance. At that point, he could view most of the harbor. If Union warships were spotted, the captain would merely steer the *Minho* out to sea, fire the boilers, and outrun the slower ships. If, on the other hand, the harbor was clear of blockade, he would dock the ship, quickly unload the goods, and be away in a matter of just a few hours.

As the *Minho* rounded the western tip of Sullivans Island, the captain, along with the lookouts, examined the boat traffic around Charleston, approximately three-and-a-half miles away. At first, they did not detect the small fleet of Federal warships lying less than a mile to their starboard and near the northern tip of Sullivans Island.

Moments later, a lookout spotted the Union gunboats and sounded a warning, but as the captain turned the ship toward the Atlantic, three more Federal ships were spotted approaching from the south, effectively cutting off escape. Realizing there was no chance for flight, and fearing the fate of the crew as captives of the Federal army, the captain of the *Minho* pointed the vessel toward Bowman's Jetty, a six-hundred-foot long ridge of partially submerged rocks extending into Charleston Harbor from Sullivans Island. Moments later, amid the noise of shattering hull plates, the *Minho* slammed into the rocks and skidded onto the top of the ridge. The ship's officers and crew quickly abandoned the ship, leaping into the surrounding water and swimming to the nearby shore.

Now completely unmanned and with large gaping holes in the hull, the *Minho* rapidly took on water and settled onto the jetty rocks.

Because of the war and the growing presence of Union troops and ships in the area, no immediate attempt was made to recover any of the cargo aboard the *Minho*. When Fraiser, Trenholm, and Company learned that the original consignment was virtually intact, they requested and received permission to make a salvage attempt.

After spending several weeks trying to refloat the *Minho*, the owners finally decided it was not possible. Days after abandoning the project, they sold the vessel, along with its entire contents, for only six thousand dollars. The new owners, a group of Charleston businessmen, recovered approximately seventy-five percent of the cargo and, during the next few weeks, auctioned it to Charleston residents.

For just over ten years, the wrecked *Minho* remained lodged on the rock of the jetty. Inside the fractured, water-filled hull, a great deal of the original cargo remained untouched. Several crates of Enfield rifles were among the unrecovered goods. In 1873, the U.S. Army Corps of Engineers, while modifying Bowman's Jetty, pulled the *Minho*'s remains from its position and allowed it to settle onto the bottom of the harbor.

During the early 1980s, South Carolina's Institute of Archeology and Anthropology became interested in the historical significance of three sunken ships near Bowman's Jetty, one being the *Minho*. In December 1985, the institute issued a salvage license that permitted recovery of lost cargo from the remains of the vessels. During the process, divers working around the hulk of the *Minho* discovered a case of twenty rifles. After the long-submerged firearms came to the surface, they were identified as Enfields. Based on some concentrated research, it was eventually learned that the case was part of a secret shipment carried by the *Minho* and intended for Confederate troops.

Several days later, a second crate of Enfields was recovered near the wreck. Scattered about the bottom sands of the harbor next to the crate were more than one thousand bullets.

Interest in the *Minho*'s rifle shipment increased, and during the next two years several more full crates of the weapons were discovered. Divers also recovered more than one thousand six hundred bullets.

Salvage activity was postponed during the 1987-88 winter storm season, and when it was resumed in April 1988, divers were delighted to discover that storm-generated currents had surged through the *Minho*'s interior, cleaning it of a heavy deposit of sand. During the first dive, two more crates of rifles were discovered along with hundreds more bullets. Over the next few days, three more full cases of Enfields were located. Because of equipment difficulties, not all of the crates were brought to the surface.

Salvage and recovery operations slowed down after 1989 when Hurricane Hugo struck the region. As a result of the storm, millions of tons of sand were shifted around the bottom of the harbor, much of it covering the *Minho*. During subsequent dives to the wreck, more crates of rifles were located, but none could be raised. Since that time, the ever-shifting sands and the termination of salvage licenses have inhibited further discovery and recovery activities.

No one knows for certain how many crates of Enfield rifles were originally aboard the *Minho* when it slammed onto Bowman's Jetty or how many still remain at the bottom of the harbor. Experts estimate it may be as many as one hundred. These rifles, Civil War artifacts more than a hundred years old, in good condition, would bring high prices from serious collectors. Offers for some of the recovered Enfields have already exceeded $1,500 apiece. With these factors, the estimated value of the rifles is well over one million dollars.

GEORGIA

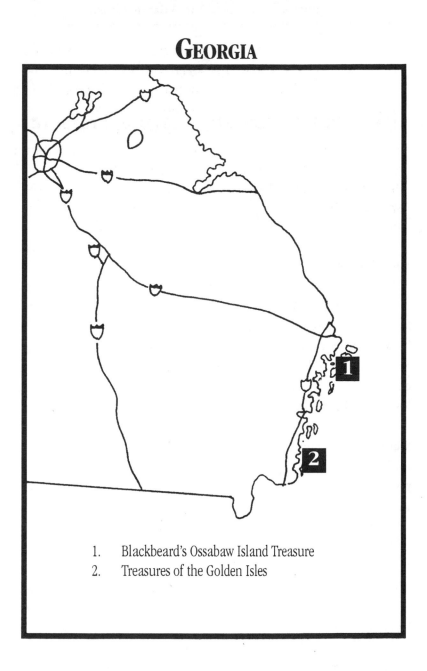

Blackbeard's Ossabaw Island Treasure

Ossabaw Island is an uninhabited, low, swampy island separated from the Georgia mainland by Bear River and the Florida Passage. Though quite unimpressive as Atlantic coastal islands go, Ossabaw Island may contain one of the largest treasures ever buried by Blackbeard.

So much time has passed since the glory days of piracy up and down the Atlantic Coast that the actual facts behind many of the fascinating tales of lost, sunken, and buried treasures may never be known. Entering the realm of folktale and legend, tales of pirates, their raids and buried treasures have fascinated people for centuries, and the mysteries associated with their reportedly huge lost treasure troves have tantalized readers for ages.

A number of Blackbeard's piratical activities have been documented, but so much of his life and career has transformed into folklore. It may be argued that more fabulous tales surround the pirate Blackbeard than any other brigand who raided and pillaged this part of the Atlantic coast. One such story circulates about his alleged treasure cache on Ossabaw Island, Georgia.

As the story goes, Blackbeard, following a series of successful raids on several merchant vessels along the Carolina coast, found his fleet of three ships pursued by four privateers. The officers and crew of these well-armed ships, commissioned by a consortium of businessmen and traders who suffered great losses to Blackbeard and other brigands, were highly paid to eliminate piracy in and around the major shipping lanes. Aware that the small and highly maneuverable privateers were gaining on them, Blackbeard signaled for his ships to sail a different route, thus splitting the pursuit. Two of the pirate vessels veered off southeastward into the open Atlantic Ocean while Blackbeard's ship continued along a course paralleling the South Carolina coast. Two of the privateers chased the southeastward-bound pirate vessels, while the other two continued in pursuit of the pirate leader.

Though Blackbeard's ship was the fastest vessel of his fleet, it was no match for the privateers that moved steadily closer. In addition to being a much larger and heavier ship, Blackbeard's vessel was heavily packed with booty taken from previous raids. Lying dangerously low in the water, the hull of the pirate ship was filled with at least a dozen wooden casks filled with gold ingots.

Realizing he would not be able to outrun the privateers, Blackbeard chose instead to outwit them. During the dark of night, Blackbeard commanded his navigator to turn into Ossabaw Sound, a shallow body of water that separated Pine Island from Ossabaw Island along Georgia's northern coast. As the pirate ship lay deep in the sound, the pursuing privateers, unaware they had been given the slip, continued southward along the Georgia coast. On the following morning before sailing out into the open Atlantic, Blackbeard ordered his crew to put in at nearby Bradley Point, the northeastern tip of Ossabaw Island. The pirates were in need of a fresh-water supply, and Blackbeard knew of a pond about two hundred yards inland beyond the point. After anchoring offshore, Blackbeard went ashore with the crewmen, who would fill the water barrels.

As the barrels were carried toward the fresh-water pond, Blackbeard remained on Bradley Point. Examining his vessel in deep anchorage offshore, the pirate was surprised to see how deep she sat in the water. Blackbeard was concerned that the weight of the accumulated treasure would slow down the ship so much that it might be overtaken by pursuers. Then and there, he decided to lighten the load by removing some of the casks of gold from the ship and burying them on Bradley Point.

With the help of several crewmen and two prisoners taken during an earlier raid, fifteen casks were lifted from the hull, loaded into the rowboat, and taken to shore. Several trips were necessary, and by the time all were finally delivered to the site selected by Blackbeard, it was dusk.

While the pirates stood by, the two prisoners dug a trench five-feet deep and twenty-feet long. The work was difficult for the tired and hungry captives, and when they stopped to rest, one or more of the pirates would step forward and lash them with a whip.

When the trench was completed, the casks were rolled in, and the prisoners commenced filling the excavation. With about eighteen inches of dirt left to completely bury the treasure trove, three pirates suddenly pulled their pistols from their sashes and shot the two unfortunate prisoners, killing them instantly. The bodies were rolled into the trench, and the pirates kicked the remaining dirt atop them.

The next morning, Blackbeard's ship, considerably lighter without the heavy gold-filled casks, sailed out of Ossabaw Sound and toward more adventure. Blackbeard, according to the prevailing tales, never returned to recover his Ossabaw Island treasure.

In 1957, two residents of Savannah, Georgia, were fishing in Ossabaw Sound when they decided to put ashore at Bradley Point.

After exploring around that part of the island for about two hours, the two men were returning to their boat when they encountered a partially covered skeleton in the sand near the highest part of the point. As they brushed the sand away from the skeleton, they discovered yet another. The two men decided they had stumbled upon an old Indian grave and began to search for artifacts but found nothing. As it was getting late in the day, they returned to their boat.

Months later, the two fishermen related their discovery to a friend who, in turn, told it to another. Eventually, the story made its way to a historian steeped in Atlantic Coast pirate lore who immediately connected the two skeletons to the tale of Blackbeard's buried treasure.

The historian finally arranged a trip to be taken by boat from Savannah Harbor to Ossabaw Island. Upon arriving, however, he could not find the skeletons. Though he explored every inch of Bradley Point, he found no sign of them. Later, he explained that the numerous oceanic storms that commonly hit this area likely covered the skeletons with sand or washed them away completely. Even the low ridge of Bradley Point changes over time with erosion and deposition, according to coastal geomorphologists.

To date, no discovery of Blackbeard's fifteen casks of gold bars have ever been recorded, and most researchers are convinced they still lie buried somewhere on Bradley Point.

Treasures of the Golden Isles

The truth behind many of the tales and legends of lost and sunken treasures on and off Georgia's Atlantic Coast will likely never be known. In fact, a large number of treasure discoveries along Georgia's beaches remain great mysteries that flavor occasional discoveries with a strong element of the unknown.

One of the reasons for the relatively scarce knowledge of many lost Georgia coastal hoards is probably related to the fact that during the days of great pirate activity in this region, Georgia was, for the most part, uninhabited. Many scholars believe that the lack of settlements may have originally been attractive to pirates seeking desolate locations to hide stolen booty. Many pirates, after burying their treasures in remote locations on Georgia's islands, were unable to return for them for many reasons, including untimely death and unexpected capture. Many of those treasures that lay hidden or cached in areas with little or no human occupation stand little chance of ever being discovered.

As parts of some of the Georgia offshore islands gradually grow more and more attractive to residents and vacationers alike, however, the likelihood that some long lost cache may accidentally be discovered is enhanced.

Some important discoveries, in fact, have already been made. For example, in recent years, several significant coin finds have been reported on Cumberland Island, Jekyll Island, and St. Simons Island. The coins, a variety of denominations of gold and silver, all bear mint dates from the early 1700s. There is an excellent possibility that they were washed ashore from the wrecks of several Spanish ships sunk offshore in 1733.

The Spanish fleet of 1733 consisted of a group of Spanish sailing vessels transporting Mexican and South American gold—coins and ingots—to the Spanish homeland. After rendezvousing in Havana, Cuba, for several weeks while taking on supplies and making necessary repairs, the fleet then traveled northward along the Atlantic Coast toward the more favorable winds and currents of higher latitudes.

A fierce hurricane struck the fleet of 1733 shortly after leaving Havana. Though most of the ships were sunk along the Florida coast, there is strong evidence that a few were blown northward as far as the southern Georgia coast and sunk within one to two miles from shore.

Today, little remains of these vessels that have lain on the continental shelf for more than two hundred and fifty years, and their cargo has long been stirred about the ocean bottom from thousands of storms and strong currents. Lighter objects such as coins and some personal items are more easily washed up onto the shore and often discovered by vacationers.

Occasionally, a significant treasure is found. On Sapelo Island, a winter storm eroded a large portion of beach and in the process uncovered sixty gold ingots. The ingots had been stacked like cordwood three feet in the beach sand. Each of the ingots, possibly Spanish, bore the mark of the Christian cross. When the ingots were buried, by whom, and why still remains a mystery.

On St. Catherines Island, a treasure chest was dug up in 1944. Following the directions on a map that was accidently discovered between the pages of an old book in a Boston library, a man named William Gunn traveled to the north point of St. Catherines Island and excavated the chest. The chest was reportedly filled with gold and silver coins along with some jewelry and uncut emeralds.

Gunn claimed the map provided no information whatsoever on who might have buried the treasure or when it was buried.

From time to time, one hears of a buried treasure tale on the Georgia islands that carries with it some historical documentation.

There may be close to one hundred thousand dollars in currency buried in the sands on the northern point of Jekyll Island. Following a bank holdup in Savannah, Georgia, during the early 1950s, the three robbers fled southward by automobile to Brunswick, a small inlet town. They loaded their loot into a motorboat rented the previous day and traveled across the sound to Jekyll Island where they were to meet some companions waiting just offshore in a large sailboat. After transferring the holdup money into the larger boat, they all planned to sail to Jamaica.

Arriving at Jekyll Island, the robbers were dismayed to discover neither the getaway boat nor their companions were there. All that night and part of the next day, they waited hopefully for their partners, but as time passed, hope for a successful escape began to dim.

Meanwhile, law enforcement authorities had tracked the robbers to Brunswick. Upon arriving, they learned from a dock employee that three men matching the descriptions of the robbers had rented a motorboat for "fishing"on Jekyll Island. Moments later, lawmen in three boats were motoring across the sound toward the island.

As the lawmen approached Jekyll Island, the robbers, waiting along the northern point, spotted them in the distance. Immediately, the robbers excavated a hole in the sand, dropped in the loot, and covered it up. Following that, they pulled the motorboat into a grove of trees and fled on foot southward along the shore.

After landing their boats on the island about thirty minutes later, the lawman followed the drag marks of the rented motorboat and found it within minutes. Spotting the footprints of the robbers in the sand, the policemen took off in pursuit, eventually overtaking the tired and hungry fugitives who were arrested and returned to Savannah.

The three robbers was sentenced to prison. During the trial, however, the money's location was never revealed, and the convicted men vowed to one another to reunite after being released and return together for the buried money on Jekyll Island.

Two of the robbers died in prison. One succumbed to pneumonia during the first year of incarceration; the second died when he was accidentally hit in the head by a piece of falling metal. The third robber was paroled after twelve years. Following his release, he went to live with his sister in North Carolina for a few weeks. After the short visit, the ex-convict planned to return to Jekyll Island and recover the money. While hitchhiking to his sister's house, he was hit by a car and died several days later in a Columbia, South Carolina, hospital. Before he died the man told an intern about the bank robbery, the escape, and the buried money. To date, it has never been found.

There is a distinct possibility that other treasures of unknown origin lie in the beach sands of Georgia's many offshore islands.

FLORIDA

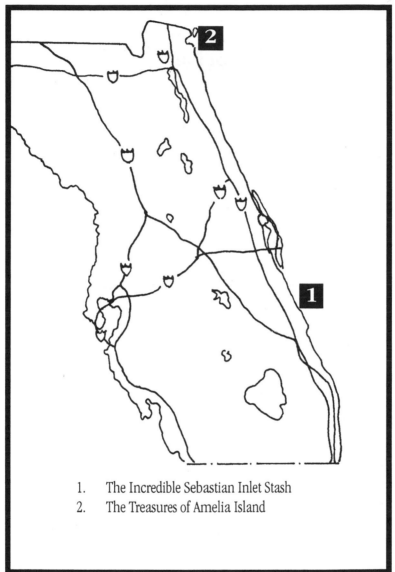

1. The Incredible Sebastian Inlet Stash
2. The Treasures of Amelia Island

The Incredible Sebastian Inlet Stash

On July 24, 1715, eleven Spanish ships, each one loaded with a king's ransom in treasure, sailed from Havana harbor. The vessels carried gold, silver, and precious stones from the many Spanish-held mines in Mexico and South America, finely crafted jewelry, and other valuable goods such as china, golden chalices, and candleholders. As the ships paralleled the North American shore along the east coast of Florida, a hurricane struck. Ten ships were either sunk or blown upon sandbars by the high winds, and the great treasures transported by each were either lost or nearly impossible to retrieve. Only one vessel survived the storm and returned to Spain.

What many believe to be the greatest concentration of the treasure carried by the 1715 Spanish fleet, an amount estimated to be worth many millions of dollars, was accumulated on a sandbar near Sebastian Inlet. While much of this treasure has been recovered, untold portions remain buried in the sands.

At least four treasure-laden vessels belonging to what the Spanish called the Plate Fleet of 1715 wrecked near Sebastian Inlet. Miraculously, most of the ships' officers and crew survived the disaster and managed to swim or float to the nearby barrier island shore. Suspecting it might be a long time before they would be rescued, the survivors constructed crude shelters using the ship's planks that had floated to shore.

A single longboat survived the disaster, and after some deliberation, a handful of officers and crew were selected to row back to Havana and alert authorities of the disaster. Two weeks later, a relief and rescue expedition left Havana and arrived a few days later just off Sebastian Inlet. Sergeant Solarzano, who was placed in charge of the expedition, delivered to the survivors a set of orders from the Cuban governor: for the next two years they were to remain encamped at this location while they salvaged the treasure from the wrecked ships. From time to time, relief ships would delivered supplies and eventually ships would arrive from Spain to retrieve some of the treasure.

Though inexperienced in underwater recovery, the survivors labored diligently, and as the months passed they succeeded in bringing tons of recovered gold and silver ingots, chests filled with precious stones and jewelry, and other valuable cargo to shore. While diving for treasure many of the Spaniards lost their lives in the treacherous surf.

On shore, a separate storeroom built from salvaged ship timbers served to house the recovered treasure. Before the end of the first year, the structure was nearly filled to its seven-foot roof.

Eighteen months following the wreck of the Plate Fleet, a Spanish ship arrived at Sebastian Inlet to transport the first shipment of salvaged treasure to Spain. More ships, it was promised, were to arrive in the months ahead to deliver supplies and pick up more cargo.

As the months passed, word of the wreck of the 1715 fleet spread to all the major Atlantic ports. Henry Jennings, a highly successful pirate with a small fleet of ships, learned about the large Spanish treasure near Sebastian Inlet while docked at a port on the west African coast. He immediately began to make plans to take it. With the Spaniards recovering the sunken valuables and bringing them to a central location on the beach it would be an easy matter, thought Jennings, to simply storm the camp, remove the treasure, and leave. He was correct.

From his spies, Jennings learned that the treasure storehouse was almost filled, and that within a few weeks, two more Spanish ships were expected to arrive and obtain the accumulated treasure. Taking three hundred well-armed and experienced fighting men, Jennings led an attack on the Sebastian Inlet treasury. Soon, all of the guards were killed. Camp residents, on hearing the commotion, fled to another part of the beach and watched helplessly as the pirates loaded the treasure into longboats.

Despite filling three ships with captured treasure, Jennings could only remove half of what had been gathered in the storehouse. Dangerously overloaded, he sailed his small fleet from the area.

The Spaniards were in great fear of Jennings and worried that he would return for another raid. Taking what provisions they could carry, they fled southward, abandoning the ongoing salvage efforts as well as the camp. The two Spanish ships expected to arrive to take back the accumulated treasure became lost and never reached Sebastian Inlet. Untended, the camp soon fell into disarray. Tropical storms destroyed the structures, and ocean waves gradually deposited sands onto the camp's remains during the next two centuries. Eventually, the Spanish authorities forgot the remaining treasure salvaged from the four ships of the 1715 fleet.

In 1955, a strong hurricane slammed the eastern Florida coast, causing massive destruction. Along the beaches near Sebastian Inlet, more than fifteen feet of sand was displaced. At the ancient camp of the 1715 fleet survivors, the storm uncovered an amazing collection of Spanish treasure: gold and silver coins, golden church relics, including crosses and chalices, broken clay and china pots and dishes, jewelry, exquisite stones, cannonballs, and several ship artifacts.

A nearby resident named Kip Wagner, after stumbling onto this rich cache of treasure, began combing the area with a metal detector. Wagner found so many Spanish coins that he eventually began to refer to the region as the "money beach." Although Wagner wasn't aware of it then, he had accidentally stumbled onto the campsite of the Plate Fleet survivors and a portion of what remained of their storehouse treasure. Curious about his discovery, Wagner subsequently invested a great deal of time and effort in researching the origin of the treasure.

Wagner soon learned about the Plate Fleet and the 1715 hurricane disaster. Realizing the possibility of more ships and their treasures only a few feet under the water and just a few hundred of yards offshore, he organized a team of divers, archaeologists, and salvers. He obtained a salvage lease from the state of Florida, and in a short time located two of the wrecks. From these sunken vessels, Wagner recovered more than one million dollars' worth of gold coins, and ingots, jewelry, Chinese porcelain, silver platters, and several ornamental chains made of pure gold.

When Wagner retired from the treasure recovery business in 1965, he estimated at least six million dollars' worth of treasure still lay on the ocean bottom not far from Sebastian Inlet.

The Treasures of Amelia Island

Amelia Island, located in the northeastern corner of Florida's Nassau County, is a popular resort area these days with fine hotels, professional golf courses, and a myriad of tourist attractions. Prior to arriving, few vacationers who visit Amelia Island are aware that it was once a favored hiding place for pirates, or that noted brigand Louis Aury once cached $60,000 worth of gold coins here, a loot for which he never returned and that remains lost to this day.

A Frenchman, Aury was born in 1787 to a family of poor fishermen, so he readily took to the sea. Young Aury soon grew bored with fishing, however, and early in life developed an acute longing for adventure. When he was fifteen years old, Aury left home and obtained passage on a trading ship that crossed the Atlantic Ocean, visited several ports along the east coast, and finally docked at the port of New Orleans.

In New Orleans, Aury met Jean Lafitte, likely the most famous pirate of the time. Attracted by Lafitte's poise and zest for life, Aury asked to become a member of his crew. After demonstrating impressive skills in all phases of sailing and vessel maintenance, young Aury often pleaded with Lafitte to allow him to become one of his fighting men and to be included in the numerous raids launched by the pirate leader.

Admiring Aury's pluck, Lafitte eventually allowed the young Frenchman to accompany him on raids of merchant ships and small coastal communities. Aury soon began to distinguish himself in battle. Fearless, an excellent fighter, and unwilling to offer or accept surrender, Aury worked himself into Lafitte's favor. Eventually, citing his fighting spirit and leadership qualities, Lafitte appointed Aury as captain of one of his ships. During the years that followed, Aury impressed Lafitte, and he was responsible for many daring predations on merchant vessels both in the Atlantic Ocean and Caribbean Sea.

After the War of 1812, Lafitte and others like him were offered pardons for their piracy crimes. Many, including Lafitte, were growing tired of the constant pursuit and harassment from the authorities and craved the peace and serenity of a simple life. Since most of the pirates had, by this time, acquired millions in gold and silver coins and ingots, along with chests of jewelry and other valuables, they were quite content to retire to a life of luxury.

Other pirates, including Aury, found greater satisfaction and adventure on the open sea than in a sedentary life on shore. Assembling his own crew, Aury sailed to Mexico where he eventually obtained a privateer's commission. Selecting Amelia Island as his base of operations, Aury constructed a small fortification near Fernandina, the old Spanish city, claimed the island as his own personal property, and raised the Mexican flag. Shortly after arriving at Amelia Island, Aury buried a wooden chest filled with $60,000 worth of gold coins.

From Amelia Island, Aury sailed out into the Atlantic and Caribbean and indiscriminately attacked and pillaged any and all ships he came in contact with.

Aury's reputation and piratical activities did not escape the notice of American authorities. After learning of Aury's stronghold on Amelia Island, the United States government wasted no time in sending a navy warship under the command of Captain J.E. Henry to remove the pirates from the island. On arriving at Amelia Island and finding Aury in residence, Henry requested an audience with the pirate. Henry, a large man, towered over the small Frenchman. With a deep voice accompanied with a stern glare, Henry told Aury he had twenty-four hours to abandon his stronghold and move off the island. Pointing to the heavily armed naval vessel anchored just offshore, Henry told Aury that if he and his fellow brigands were not gone at the end of that time, the fortification would be shelled.

Realizing he was outmanned and outgunned, Aury agreed to the only sensible action: he told Henry he would vacate the island. Turning to his crew that had gathered behind him, Aury shouted orders to evacuate immediately.

Watched closely by Henry and several U.S. sailors, Aury and his men quickly transferred their belongings to the pirate vessel anchored offshore and fled southward toward the Caribbean. According to Henry, at no time did Aury dig up his gold coins. Though Henry and several members of his crew searched the area, the treasure cache was never found. Aury never returned to Amelia Island to recover his treasure, and researchers are convinced the coin-filled chest remains buried somewhere near the old city of Fernandina.

As the years passed and this part of the American coast became more settled, the stories of pirate Aury's hidden treasure on Amelia Island enticed many to search for it. Interestingly though, Aury's chest was never found; other treasures, likely those of other pirates who occasionally used the island, were discovered.

In 1748, the Spanish vessel *Halcon*, transporting a shipment of gold and silver coins, sank in adjacent Nassau Sound. The wreck's location has been pinpointed in recent years, but archaeologists working at the site claim the ship is entirely covered with sand and silt and that the cost of removing this overburden could run as much as $250 million.

Records show that in 1795 the Spanish vessel *Santa Barbara*, believed to have been carrying several kegs of gold coins, sank within two miles of Amelia Island.

It is also a matter of record that the British ship *Betsey* went down off the eastern shore of Amelia Island in 1812. In the ship's hold was ten thousand dollars' worth of gold coins—all worth considerably more today.

The *Nicholas Adolph*, a Swedish merchant vessel, sank in shallow water near Amelia Island's north shore. The ship was carrying a safe filled with money that would purchase sugar in the Caribbean Islands. Though the wreck of the *Nicholas Adolph* has been located, the safe has never been found.

During the 1890s, a strange story concerning the discovery of a large cache of coins near present-day Fort Clinch State Park circulated throughout the area. According to the tale, three men, using a map obtained from unknown sources, rowed out to a point on Amelia Island's north shore and dug up gold coins worth approximately $170,000. During the subsequent division of the treasure on the island, one of the men was killed, and the others rowed away after loading the hoard into their boat. Neither the killing nor the treasure's origin has ever been explained.

In 1920, a man searching near Fernandina dug up a metal pot filled to the top with silver coins. Two years later, several children playing in an open field discovered several gold coins, all dated in the 1700s. The owner of the field, after being shown the coins, began digging in the area and eventually recovered coins worth $20,000 dollars.

In 1933, two men found a cache of four hundred gold coins on the outskirts of Fernandina. The coins with mint dates as old as the mid-1500s were likely part of a pirate cache because they were of mixed origin—England, France, and Spain—and denomination.

Amelia Island's sandy seaward shores have yielded numerous gold and silver coins from sunken vessels. Following severe storms in the area, treasure hunters often arrive at the island's beaches by the dozens, and with the aid of metal detectors they have discovered coins worth thousands of dollars.

Glossary

- **Aft:** At or near the stern or rear of a ship.
- **Archipelago:** A group of islands; a sea studded with islands.
- **Barrier island:** An island lying parallel to shore separated from it by a sound.
- **Bay:** A wide inlet.
- **Booty:** Spoils or riches taken in war or raiding.
- **Bow:** The forepart of a ship.
- **Brigand:** A member of a band of men, usually pirates, who rob and plunder.
- **Bullion:** Gold or silver bars or ingots.
- **Buoy:** An anchored float marking a navigable channel or dangerous shallows.
- **Cache:** A hiding place for treasure; a hoard or store.
- **Caisson:** A watertight chamber normally employed in underwater work such as lifting submerged vessels.
- **Cannonade:** Small cannon.
- **Capsize:** To upset or cause to flounder, especially a boat or ship; to overturn or become overturned on water.
- **Cargo:** The freight, goods, or luggage carried by a ship.
- **Caulking:** Pitch used to make watertight the seams of a ship.
- **Constable:** A type of policeman.
- **Continental shelf:** The underwater plain located along the oceanic borders of most continents, descending in a slope toward deep water.
- **Crewman:** A man who works on a ship; part of the ship's crew.
- **Cutter:** A single-masted sailing boat rigged fore and aft.

- **First mate:** A deck officer on a merchant ship who ranks just below the captain and is responsible for carrying out his orders.

- **Flotsam:** The wreckage of a ship or its cargo found floating on the sea.

- **Fore:** The bows of a ship.

- **Fore-and-aft rig:** A sailing ship rig in which all the sails, or most of them, are set on the masts or on stays at the mid-ship line.

- **Freebooter:** Someone who lives by plunder and loot, a word often used synonymously with pirate.

- **Frigate:** A warship of five to seven thousand tons; a three-masted sailing ship carrying up to sixty guns.

- **Funnel:** The metal flue of a ship or steam engine, a smokestack.

- **Gale:** A wind having a speed from thirty-two to sixty-three miles per hour; a strong wind.

- **Galley:** A long, low, narrow single-decked ship propelled by sails and oars, often rowed by condemned criminals. Also the kitchen of a ship.

- **Golden eagles:** Ten dollar gold pieces.

- **Gunboat:** A small but heavily armed vessel of shallow draft for patrol and for shore bombardment.

- **Hawser:** A rope, or sometimes a steel cable, used in mooring a ship.

- **Hold:** The space below decks in a ship where cargo is stored.

- **Hull:** The body framework of a ship.

- **Ingot:** A lump or bar of metal, generally gold, silver, or steel, cast for ease of transport.

- **Inlet:** A narrow arm of a sea or river; a passage between islands into a lagoon, an opening, an entrance.

- **Isle:** A small island, sometimes called an islet.

- **Jetsam:** The cargo or gear thrown overboard from a ship in distress to lighten the load. It sinks or washes onto shore.

- **Keel:** The curved base of a ship's framework, extending from bow to stern.

- **Knot:** A unit of speed—one nautical mile per hour.

- **Liner:** A large passenger ship.

- **List:** To lean to one side, especially a ship.

- **Longboat:** The largest rowboat carried aboard a sailing ship.

- **Mainsail:** A sail bent to the main yard of a square-rigged vessel; a sail set to the afterpart of a mainmast in a fore-and-aft rig.

- **Man-o'-war:** A warship.

- **Mast:** A long wooden or metal pole set up on a ship's keel or deck to carry sails or other rigging.

- **Mutineer:** Someone guilty of mutiny.

- **Mutiny:** Open revolt against lawful authority, especially naval or military authority.

- **Paddle wheel:** A wheel with long boards projecting at right angles from its circumference, used to propel a boat. A common name for a type of boat propelled by a paddle wheel.

- **Piece of eight:** An obsolete Spanish coin worth eight *reales*.

- **Pier:** A wooden-decked structure supported on piles and built to extend for some distance into the sea or other body of water, used to give passengers access to vessels.

- **Pillage:** The act of taking goods by force, generally armed force.

- **Piracy:** The robbery of ships at sea.

- **Pirate:** Someone who commits piracy.

- **Port:** The side of the ship that is on the left of someone facing the bow.

- **Privateer:** An armed private vessel authorized by a government to engage in hostile acts against the enemy; the captain or a member of the crew of such a vessel.

- **Prow:** The forepart of a boat or ship; the bow.

- **Reale:** A former Spanish silver coin.

- **Rigging:** All of the ropes and chains used for supporting a ship's masts and spars and for hoisting and lowering the sails.

- **Rowboat:** A small, shallow boat propelled by oars.

- **Rudder:** A flat piece of wood or metal hinged vertically to a vessel's sternpost, used for steering.

- **Salvage:** Items rescued from shipwrecks.

- **Salvor:** One engaged in the business of salvage.

- **Sandbar:** A bank of sand built up at the mouth of a river or along the shore.

- **Schooner:** A fore-and-aft vessel with two or more masts.

- **Seafaring:** Working as a sailor; traveling on the sea.

- **Sea wall:** A wall constructed to prevent encroachment by the sea.

- **Shoal:** A part of a river, sea, or lake where the water is very shallow.

- **Skiff:** A small rowing boat.

- **Sound:** A narrow channel of water connecting two seas or a sea and a lake; a long, rather broad, ocean inlet.

- **Spit:** A shoal or reef extending from the shore.

- **Squall:** A sudden high wind, generally accompanied by rain at sea.

- **Square-rigger:** A sailing vessel, the chief sails of which extend by horizontal yards suspended from the middle.

- **Starboard:** The side of the ship that is on the right of someone facing forward.

- **Steamer:** A ship driven by steam.

- **Stern:** The rear end of a ship.

- **Steward:** A ship's officer in charge of stores and arrangements about meals; an attendant who looks after the personal needs of a ship's passengers.

- **Tiller:** The lever arm by which the rudder is turned.

- **Undercurrent:** A current below the upper surface of water.

- **Warship:** A heavily armed ship used in naval combat.

- **Watch:** A period of time, usually four hours, during which part of a ship's company is required to be on duty; a person or persons on watch duty.

- **Yard:** A cylindrical spar tapering at the ends, slung from a mast to support and spread a sail.

Selected References

Anderson, Bill, and Nina Anderson. *Southern Treasures*. Chester, Conn.: The Globe Pequot Press, 1987.

Blackstone, Kate. "Baron de Castine's Lost Fortune," *Lost Treasure*, August, 1992.

Brown, Edward. "Spanish Silver Coins of Long Beach Island," *Lost Treasure*, June, 1981.

Casey, Tim. "Amelia, Isle of Pirate Loot," *Lost Treasure*, October, 1992.

Duffy, Howard M. "Louis Aury's Lost Florida Caches," *Lost Treasure*, February, 1995.

_____. "Machias, Maine: Prime Treasure Site," *Lost Treasure*, January, 1977.

_____. "Island Treasure Guarded by a Herd of Wild Horses," *Western Treasures*, December, 1976.

_____. "New London's Ill-Fated Spanish Treasure," *Lost Treasure*, February, 1976.

_____. "The *Magnifique*'s Sunken Treasure," *True Treasure*, September-October, 1975.

_____. "Joseph Braddish's Two Pirate Treasures," *Treasure World*, June-July, 1975.

_____. "Where is the Treasure of Maine's Mad Baron?" *True Treasure*, July-August, 1975.

_____. "Black Bellamy's Lost Maine Treasure Trove," *Lost Treasure*, March-April, 1975.

Ferguson, Jeff. "Virginia's Sunken French Gold," *Lost Treasure*, July, 1978.

_____. "Lost Gold Ingots of Onslow Bay," *Lost Treasure*, December, 1977.

_____. "The Tsarist Emeralds Treasure," *Lost Treasure*, July, 1976.

_____. "Sunken Gold Off Virginia," *Lost Treasure*, December, 1975.

_____. "The Sunken Colonial Treasure Ship," *True Treasure*, July-August, 1975.

Gablehouse, Charles. "Manhattan Treasure Ship," *True Treasure*, March-April, 1968.

Getz, Donald E. "The Bankers' Shipwreck Treasure," *Treasure World*, August-September, 1972.

Henson, Michael Paul. "Maine: Myriad of Treasure," *Lost Treasure*, July, 1991.

_____. "New Jersey Treasure Sites," *Lost Treasure*, January, 1991.

Howard, Dan. "Lost Treasure of the Isles of Shoals," *Lost Treasure*, June, 1978.

Hoyt, Edwin P. *Nantucket: The Life of an Island*. Brattleboro, Vt.: The Stephen Greene Press, 1978.

Jameson, W.C. *Buried Treasures of the South*. Little Rock, Ark.: August House Publishers, Inc., 1992.

_____. "The Chatham Beach Treasure," *Lost Treasure*, November, 1991.

Kiedrowski, Leonard. "Treasures of the Nag's Head Bankers," *Treasure World*, June-July, 1970.

Krippene, Ken. "New Clues to Blackbeard's South Carolina Buried Treasure," *Treasure*, February, 1978.

Masters, Al. "Missing—Millions in $10 Golden Eagles," *True Treasure*, January-February, 1976.

_____. "Delaware's Jinxed Treasure Ship," *True Treasure*, March-April, 1971.

Matthews, Gene. "The Treasure of Sebastian Inlet," *True Treasure*, November-December, 1973.

National Geographic Society. *Undersea Treasures*. Washington, D.C.: National Geographic Society, 1974.

Paterson, J.H. *North America*. 9th Edition. New York: Oxford University Press, 1994.

Remick, Teddy. "Wreck of the Golden Eagles," *Lost Treasure*, January, 1976.

Snow, Edward Rowe. *Ghosts, Gales, and Gold*. New York: Dodd, Mead, and Co., 1972

_____. *True Tales of Buried Treasure*. New York: Dodd, Mead, and Co., 1951.

Taft, Lewis A. "A Pirate Treasure in New England," *True Treasure*, Summer, 1967.

Tower, Howard, B., Jr. "The *Minho*'s Iron Triangle," *Lost Treasure*, July, 1991.

Voynick, Stephen M. *The Mid-Atlantic Treasure Coast*. Wallingford, Pa.: The Middle Atlantic Press, 1984.

Weinman, Ken. "Lost Pirate Treasure in Maine," *Lost Treasure*, July, 1994.

_____. "Lost Gold of Chatham Beach," *Lost Treasure*, April, 1994.

Williams, Carlos. "Has The Lost Byfield Treasure Been Recovered?" *Lost Treasure*, April, 1992.

Williams, Jerry. *Treasure Hunter: Undiscovered Treasures of the Southeast*. Orangeburg, S.C.: Sandlapper Publishing Company, Inc., 1992.

Williams, Larry R. and Juanita H. Williams. "East Coast Sea Treasure," *Lost Treasure*, September, 1994.